TWO FEET UNDER

Douglas John Knox

Copyright © Douglas John Knox 2022.
First Published 2022 by Douglas John Knox
Northumberland, England

The rights of Douglas John Knox to be identified as the author of this work has been asserted in accordance with the Copyright, Designs and Patents Act of 1988

All rights reserved; no part of this publication may be reproduced, stored in a retrieval system, or transmitted in any form. electronic, mechanical, photocopying, recording or otherwise without the consent of the author, or a license permitting copy in the UK issued by the Copyright Licensing Agency Ltd. www.cla.co.uk
All the characters in this book are fictitious and any resemblance to any living person is purely coincidental.

ISBN: 9798355654085

Cover Photos: Pixabay.
Cover Design: Douglas John Knox

Email: douglasjohnknox@gmail.com
Facebook: @douglasjohnknox
Twitter @douglasjohn_k

TWO FEET UNDER

Max Cornell is detective chief inspector in charge of Northumberland's murder investigation team and never far from controversy. It is while his superiors are considering discipline over his conduct at a recent crown court hearing, a climate change activist is murdered in a small Northumberland village.

All fingers point towards a farmer who has been the subject of recent protests organised by this individual. Cornell, however, is not convinced the farmer is the perpetrator, but he is faced with a village hiding a secret and villagers refusing to talk. To find a link to the murderer Cornell is compelled to investigate the disappearance of a visitor to the village two years before.

Douglas John Knox's latest novel is an intricate tale of obsession and tragedy, sprinkled with humour.

TWO FEET UNDER

CHAPTER ONE

How Amy Carter found his personal email address, Max could only speculate. She had once worked for MI5 but living in the USA for fifteen years, it seemed unlikely she would still have UK contacts, or access to the technology. Yet she had emailed him and not for the first time.

Max ran his fingers through his long, almost black, curly hair and wondered about his onetime lover. They had first met when he worked for Scotland Yard's anti-terror unit, their paths crossing during a major covert operation in the heart of London.

They had worked well together, socialised well together, moved in together, had a son together and Max had thought their life together was good. But then after two years and without any notice, Amy departed for the USA taking their son with her, choosing to live with a CIA agent named Carter, whom she had been seeing behind Max's back and who had been recalled to his US base.

To put it mildly, Max had not taken her desertion very well and went on a drinking spree that lasted for months until his superintendent saved him from self-destruction. Fortunately, he had not fully succumbed to alcohol and was able to stop drinking with only a little difficulty.

Much had happened to him since then; working in serious crime in the North West, married, widowed, and a move to Tyne and Wear. He had rarely thought of his ex-lover Amy, until she and their son, Todd, turned up on his doorstep six months ago. Max had questioned himself since as to why he did not answer the door and embrace his son during the Carter's visit to his Cullercoats home during their UK vacation, but he hadn't liked what he saw through the lounge window. The tall, well-built boy standing in his garden drinking from a can and chewing gum with the ferocity of a NFL coach, did not touch his heartstrings. When he received the DNA results a few days later, he discovered why that was.

Now he was reading the second email he'd received from Amy in six months concerning Todd, whom, at the time she left him fifteen years ago, Max had thought was his son.

The first communication from her had requested Max contribute to Todd's further education in America. Max had declined for two reasons. One, he didn't think he should have to pay for Todd to play basketball and two, Todd wasn't his son.

His reply then was along those lines, with an explanation of how he had obtained Todd's DNA from the Red Bull can Todd had left on Max's gate post during their visit. He could send Amy the results of the test if she required it, but he was sure she would know fine well Max was not Todd's father.

Cornell thought his response would have been the end of the correspondence, but to his astonishment he had received another email from Amy this morning.

Some of it was garbled, some parts confused, and Max wondered whether Amy had been drinking before she wrote it. She had always liked a drink.

"You believed Todd to be your son for all of his life, therefore you have a parental duty to contribute to his further education."

The email continued with the threat of court action in both the USA and UK if Max did not comply.

He wondered if Amy was actually taking legal advice. He couldn't believe a lawyer, of any nationality, would advise her to sue him for college fees for her son, who was not his.

He should ignore the email. He was going to, but he just couldn't resist replying.

"Amy, your request has given a whole new meaning to the phrase, 'clutching at straws'."

Thinking of Amy made him think of Michelle. He hadn't thought of his dead wife recently and felt guilty about that. She was a Manchester girl and a police sergeant. They had only been married for a year when Max was warned off by the North West's criminal supremo not to get too close to his business enterprises. "*Back off*," was the message, which Max ignored. Then Michelle was fatally shot during a raid on the criminal's HQ. "*We told you so*," was the riposte.

But Max had some reason to cheer a few months later. He remembered with clarity the moment the jury brought in the guilty verdict and the crime boss physically staggered on hearing it. He staggered some more three weeks later when he was sentenced to thirty years. Michelle's death was avenged, a little.

His thoughts were interrupted by the spectacle of his dog, Rex, observed from the corner of his eye, sitting quietly at the side of the desk with his leash in his mouth, waiting patiently to go for a walk.

Max laughed and gave the big German Shepherd a good stroke and scratch around the ears.

'Not long now, lad. Mabel and Marian will be here soon.'

Rex had been his neighbour's dog. An elderly lady who had bought a pup for company, not appreciating the size of a pup's paws was usually indicative of its adult size. When she died, Max was given the dog by her son. Now a two year old, Rex had grown much larger than any German Shepherd had a right to grow.

Max got up from his seat and made a cup of coffee. He took it into the lounge where he could see his guests arrive through the front window. The same window he had observed the boy he once thought was his and knew immediately he saw him, he wasn't.

And now his thoughts turned to Dr Mabel Wainwright, senior forensics pathologist for Newcastle and Northumberland, his girlfriend, whom he knew wanted a closer relationship than the one they had. Max didn't know what he wanted, but he genuinely liked Mabel.

She and her daughter, Marian, were visiting Max Cornell's home that evening, a visit arranged by text early afternoon. Mabel wished to advise Max of information she had received that morning concerning the upcoming Symonds trial. Information that affected them both. Now that the preliminaries were completed, next Monday was the start of the much awaited murder trial.

A long walk along Whitley Bay beach followed by a Chinese takeout had been agreed at Marian's request.

Max and Mabel had become friends during the Symonds murder investigation and their relationship had progressed since, albeit slowly.

Mabel loved Max. She so desperately wanted to tell him, but was seriously worried that he would not reciprocate. Although he was caring and loving, reliable, unless work intervened, he wore a permanent smile making it difficult to judge his moods. She hoped the relationship would develop towards marriage or at least partnership status, but she was concerned how he would react if she suggested it. He rarely expressed his feelings and had a tendency to walk away from conflict when it involved himself. She worried he would walk away from her if a closer relationship was not what he wanted.

Then there was Marian who at sixteen was not yet considered sufficiently adult by her mother to be deserted, which placed an additional restriction on Max and Mabel's association growing at a faster pace.

Rex, now standing on his hind legs looking out of the lounge window suddenly dropped down on all fours at the sound of car doors closing and barked as he ran to the front door. He knew who was going to appear on the other side. Max opened the door, but was barged aside by the big German Shepherd who was intent on greeting his second best friend, Marian Wainwright. Max followed him out of the door to greet his guests.

TWO FEET UNDER

Mabel stood to one side. The dog troubled her. She was fine when Rex was asleep, or walking ahead, but she kept close contact to a minimum, not least because his brush of a tail could seriously hurt in a frenzied spell of wagging.

'Can I take him on ahead, Max?' asked Marian, giving her mother's male friend a brief hug of greeting.

'Sure. Rex, go and get your leash.'

The dog bounded back into the house, returning seconds later with the leash in his mouth. Marian took it from him and secured it to the dog's collar.

'See you both later,' she said, heading off along the promenade towards Whitley bay beach, the dog proudly trotting alongside her.

'How does that animal understand what you are saying?' asked Mabel as they watched her daughter and dog disappear into the distance.

'He doesn't. It's only the word leash he understands and associates it with walks, which he loves. If you said you were going to smash him over the head with his leash, he would still go and get it. Hang on, I'll get my coat.'

Max returned indoors and took a light jacket from one of the coat hooks inside the hall. Mabel was already outside the gate.

'Hurry up, Max, we need to catch Marian up.'

'You worry too much about the girl. Let her have some freedom.'

'She's still just sixteen, Max.'

'That's adult these days. I don't think for one moment she's in any danger while she's got Rex with her.'

'Perhaps not. You're right. I should let go a little.'

Linking Max's arm, Mabel immediately forgot her decision to give Marian more space and walked at a quicker pace, almost dragging Max along to catch up with her daughter.

By the time they reached the beach, Marian and the dog were still well ahead, she, throwing small branches of seaweed for Rex to retrieve.

'You left a message for me, Mabel. Something I needed to know about the trial,' said Max taking off his shoes.

'Yes,' she replied, 'I tried to ring you this afternoon.'

'I was in a meeting with the chief. So what's it all about?'

'I had a call from Symonds' solicitors, Marshall, Franks and Bedwell-Sloan, this morning.'

'Oh, what did they want? Changing their plea to guilty?' asked Max.

'If only. No, the defence are going to bring up our relationship,' said Mabel.

Max stopped in his tracks and faced his companion.

'Seriously?'

'That's what they said. Claimed they were being courteous by informing us in advance,' said Mabel.

'Are they going to suggest that the two of us got together to pervert the course of justice in order to frame Symonds?'

'It seems like it. I'm not sure they've got anything else?' Mabel queried.

'They haven't. I've been waiting for them to change their plea and save everyone a great deal of time.'

'It appears they have gone to some length to gather information about us, because they also mentioned us being seen in Berwick together last month.'

'So, that's the reason,' Max responded.

'What do you mean? The reason for what?'

Max stopped walking and turned Mabel around to face him.

'Look over my left shoulder. See that young guy leaning over the railings just outside the Rendezvous Café?'

'Yes, what about him?'

'He's the same guy who followed us to Berwick.'

She stared at him incredulously.

'How do you know that?' she asked.

'I recognise him from then and he's not very good,' explained Max, 'else he wouldn't be leaning on those railings.'

'What do you mean? Stop talking in riddles, Max.'

'Why would a young man like him be leaning on railings and looking out over an almost empty beach at half past seven on a warm summer's evening?'

'Perhaps he's got something on his mind,' suggested Mabel.

'Yes, it's us. Come here. Let's give him something to report back on.'

Max grabbed her in an embrace and kissed her passionately.

'Hey, you two,' shouted Marian who had returned from distance with Rex who was dragging a huge branch of seaweed behind him. The big dog dropped the end of it at Max's feet, sat down and looked up at his master.

'And what the hell do you think I'm going to do with that?' Cornell spoke to the dog. 'It's bigger than me.'

Whatever the dog's intention, it quickly evaporated as Marian, calling his name, started to run off in front once again. The big dog loped off after her.

'You see, Max, she's still just a child,' Mabel said, then after glancing towards the Rendezvous Café, said, 'that man has gone.'

'I know,' he replied.

'How did you know he was following us? Were you trained to notice things like that?' she asked as they recommenced their walk, she linking his arm once more.

'Special Branch and Anti-Terror. It never leaves you. I can recite you the model and number of every car we passed between my house and the steps down to the beach.'

'That's worrying, Max.'

'The solicitors say anything else?' Max asked, returning to the subject of their court attendance.

'Only to tell me who the defence barristers were. Lavinia Ramsay is lead counsel.'

'Heard of her but never had the pleasure.'

'I've been cross examined by her a few times. She can be a bit of a bitch. But here's the thing,' Mabel continued. 'Her husband, who is the Town Clerk of Ecklington Town Council, is knocking off the council's secretary.'

'That's interesting. How do you know that?'

'It's common knowledge amongst the legal and medical fraternity. They usually meet up at Condon Park Hotel on Thursday afternoons.'

'And Lavinia Ramsay is happy with Mr Ramsay's philandering's? Or is she ignorant of them?'

'I think she would be hard pressed to plead ignorance after all this time. It's been going on for years. It seems a bit more than just a fling.'

'Takes all sorts I suppose. Come on, I'll race you.'

The two set off running after Marian. Max pumping his legs high like Michael Johnson and she unable to compete for laughing.

TWO FEET UNDER

CHAPTER TWO

Having waved goodbye to Mabel and Marian from his front door step, Max and Rex went inside the Cullercoats home that belonged to his mother, where he and the dog lived. It was dark outside now, but the air was still warm. The big German Shepherd, subdued after the excitement of the beach, went and sat in his bed watching Max take a can of beer from the fridge and pour the contents into a glass.

Max went into his living room to watch television. Moments later the dog followed, momentarily standing on his hindlegs to look out of the window for reasons unknown, then decided to curl up on the rug in front of the artificial flames of the gas fire.

After five minutes of surfing the channels, Cornell became disillusioned. Silly quiz programmes hosted by celebrities of questionable gender, repeat films from the nineteen fifties and sixties, and dramas about ancient Egypt and the second world war. The only live sport was golf and darts, which didn't appeal.

This is what you pay exorbitant TV subscription fees for.

He left the latter on with the sound turned down low so he could reflect on the upcoming Symonds trial while savouring his beer.

Jeremy Symonds had been the MP for Berwick and district, who, during a visit to his constituency, murdered two young prostitutes, both students. He had arranged the services of same through a sex ring, owned by a police superintendent and an eminent lawyer. DCI Cornell and his murder investigation team brought them all down. There were to be many trials to follow the murder trial of Symonds.

Cornell would be the main witness for the prosecution in all of them. It would be his testimony backed up by the indisputable DNA evidence that would send the ex-MP, a police chief and a senior barrister to prison for a long time. It seemed inevitable that the defendants would plead not guilty. They usually do, then appeal after they lose the case. The lawyers the only winners in the long run, making up elaborate stories in an attempt to sway the juries and justify their fees. He had wondered what story would be made up in Symonds' case. He hadn't thought for one moment his and Mabel's relationship would be the issue. Well, good luck with that.

Was he worried about the witness stand? He was once, as a young detective sergeant, when he had been given a rough time by the defence. He vowed then, he would only answer the questions asked and never volunteer information beyond that. That is what got him into trouble all those years ago.

Nowadays, Cornell quite enjoyed being questioned in court, especially when the defence would try to cloud his evidence. He loved the "*I put it to you*" questions, which he never answered and when prompted would say something like, "*I thought the defence were making a statement, your honour, rather than asking a question.*"

Once, a judge had gotten annoyed with him but he stood his ground and both the judge and the barristers ended up analysing the supposed question. After a few minutes debate involving the stenographer, it was decided DCI Cornell was quite right, he had not in fact been asked a question.

Few of Newcastle's police officers were aware of Cornell's previous position as an inspector in the serious crime squad based at the Met in London, but stationed in Manchester. He did not attempt to enlighten them.

After Cornell had brought down the North West's crime boss, it was inevitable that the jailed criminal would put a contract out on him. He survived the first attempt on his life, but his superiors felt it was only a matter of time before the villains would succeed, therefore a move to a less contentious part of the country was suggested.

He applied for and was successful in obtaining his current posting in his native Newcastle. He had been born only a few miles from the city, moving away when he left school.

He settled into his new post quickly, given the task of leading the Newcastle and Northumberland murder investigation team, which he welcomed. It enabled him to initiate skills and techniques he had learned in North West England when dealing with the mob and gangs.

He liked to get involved at the front end of investigations which had the added advantage of being out in the field and missing meetings. At the last meeting he attended, little was established and nothing was achieved.

His latest refusal to attend an awayday somewhere in Yorkshire was being assessed at a high level, as was his comment on a local radio station when he agreed that burglaries and theft crimes were not being properly investigated.

CHAPTER THREE

Three months before

Following the dismissal of Chief Superintendent Braithwaite for gross misconduct, DCI Max Cornell had been put in temporary charge of police operations north of the Tyne and Northumberland until the senior position could be filled. Max was not given a temporary acting title, nor did he get extra pay for it. He didn't complain, which surprised the chief constable.

However, she and human resources acted quickly and within three months Max was able to return to his own office.

Chief Superintendent Anthony Blakeshaw was a promotee from Durham constabulary. He was an imposing figure, married with three children and aged about five years older than Max's forty three, shaven headed and stockily built, standing somewhere just over six feet. His previous position as a superintendent in County Durham had been uneventful and many of the police hierarchy wondered about the promotion. He was an excellent organiser, public speaker, chair of meetings, and knew the criminal law backwards but had never displayed much aptitude for detecting the serious criminal element.

DOUGLAS JOHN KNOX

His first task in his new post was to meet with his senior staff to explain his immediate objectives and what he required of them. Cornell listened but didn't contribute to the discussion. He wasn't surprised, however, when he was invited to remain after the meeting. He knew why. The chief constable would have informed her new appointee of the unconventional police practices of DCI Max Cornell.

'I understand you are a loose cannon, chief inspector,' said the new chief superintendent from his large leather seat on the other side of the desk.

Cornell said nothing, resulting in a lengthy pause.

'Well are you?' the chief superintendent asked impatiently.

'I wasn't aware you had asked me a question, sir,' responded Cornell.

There was another less lengthy pause.

'My mistake. Let's start again. I hear your investigative techniques don't always follow the book.'

Again Cornell was silent. Then Blakeshaw realised he had once more not asked a question. He decided to change tack.

'You heard what I want from my senior officers. Do you have a problem with any of it?'

'Of course not, sir.'

'Good,' said Blakeshaw, 'let's remember that. Now then, I am increasing your immediate team here in Newcastle by a sergeant and two constables.'

'I've always been two constables short, sir. What you mean is you are appointing two constables to my team to bring it up to strength. I'm a sergeant down because Bob Harvey retired and hasn't been replaced.'

Blakeshaw was about to unleash a "*don't tell me what I mean, chief inspector,*" but stopped himself as his chief inspector was absolutely right.

'Anything further, chief inspector?' he asked.

'Yes, sir. I want DC Laura Donaldson promoted to replace Bob Harvey.'

'Not a chance. She's too young,' replied the chief superintendent.

'I wasn't aware there was a minimum age for sergeants, sir?' questioned Cornell. He was about to ask whether it was because she was a woman, which it undoubtedly was, but thought better of it.

'OK,' the chief superintendent sighed with reluctance. 'So, what's she got?'

'A degree in law, passed her sergeant's exam, intelligence, competence, initiative.'

'What about management skills?'

'Very good. She tends to take the lead amongst the detective constables, sir.'

'How does she handle sexism?'

'Gives as good as she gets,' said Cornell. 'Won't stand any nonsense.'

'OK, send your Laura Donaldson in to see me. If she passes muster, I'll consider a promotion.'

'Thank you, sir. That will mean if you promote her, I'll still be a constable down.'

The chief superintendent sighed, then his demeanour suddenly changed.

'Actually, chief inspector, that may solve a problem.'

'What do you mean, sir?'

'Of where to place someone who's been a bit naughty. That's all, chief inspector. I'll see DC Donaldson now, if she's free.'

Cornell left the chief superintendent's office and the incumbent sat back and pondered. The chief constable had explained that Cornell was an excellent detective and people manager, but bent the rules when it suited. He treat his staff as equals and they respected him greatly for it. However, he occasionally gave the impression of being disrespectful towards senior staff and you sometimes never knew if he was laughing or being serious.

Blakeshaw, although only spending a few minutes alone with the chief inspector, knew what the chief constable meant. However, in the absence of any plan he could think of at that moment, he decided to cross bridges with his chief inspector if and when he came to them.

The new appointments to the murder investigation team were Peter Owusu, a young constable of Ghanian descent with the reputation of an IT geek, and Irene Stainton from Teesside, a WPC in her late forties and recently divorced.

Owusu came to DCI Cornell's attention after Cornell had asked a traffic sergeant how one of his constables had sustained a peach of a black eye.

'Questioned PC Owusu's heritage, sir,' replied the sergeant.

'Any repercussions?' queried Cornell.

'None, sir. Owusu didn't report the incident and the officer concerned kept quiet as he would have left himself open to a racism charge. I thought the black eye and the accompanying embarrassment was punishment enough.'

'Sensible man, but don't quote me on that. You need Owusu?'

'Yes, sir. He's a good cop but I won't stand in the way of him becoming a detective, which is his ambition and what you are really asking me.'

At his interview with the chief inspector, Cornell asked PC Owusu how he handled racism.

'Ignore it mainly, sir,' the young constable replied. 'I've had it all my life to the extent it no longer bothers me.'

'What about blacking a colleague's eye?'

'Oh! He went too far, sir. He was uncomplimentary about my parents and that will not do, sir.'

'Do you meet with much racism in the force?' Cornell questioned.

'Especially in the force, sir. I'm surprised that I'm being considered for detective and I'm wondering if I'm going to become some sort of statistic.'

This comment disturbed Cornell. He had worked with black officers in London and Manchester and most were good lads and lasses, but when he thought how few were high ranking, he empathised with his new detective.

'Well let's put it this way, DC Owusu. You are in my squad because you have a good record as a constable and I need your IT skills, not because you are black. You will be treated no differently to anyone else.'

Both the new recruits were welcomed into their roles alongside present incumbents, DC's Ian Dennison and David Watkins.

The final appointee, to fill the gap left by newly promoted Detective Sergeant Laura

Donaldson, was a recently demoted uniformed sergeant.

An internal investigation following a complaint from a female constable in his command had found Sergeant Martin Fielding guilty of misogyny and racism, and dismissal was recommended. Blakeshaw, who was seconded to the disciplinary process on the retirement of a senior officer suggested leniency because the officer had a wife and two young children and take his stripes instead. The remaining members of the team reluctantly agreed, but insisted it was Blakeshaw's responsibility to find him a posting.

The chief superintendent put him under the supervision of Detective Sergeant Laura Donaldson in the murder investigation team.

Cornell was moved by his superior's benevolence on the one hand, but knew the newly promoted sergeant was being put to the test on the other.

CHAPTER FOUR

Present day

The prosecution's first witness in the Jeremy Symonds murder trial was forensic pathologist Doctor Mabel Wainwright. The CPS prosecutor asked of her position, qualifications and experience, then sought testimony as to how Margaret Whitfield and Sadie Tomkinson, both sex workers, had died. Much time was spent on how the six feet six height of the perpetrator was established.

After a morning of questioning then a lunch break, Lavinia Ramsay for the defence stood.

'The defence is not denying Jeremy Symonds is six feet six inches tall, Dr Wainwright, but have you any idea of how many men in this country are of that height?'

Mabel Wainwright was very experienced at being cross examined and disliked being challenged.

'I imagine there are hundreds of thousands, but only one has the DNA of Jeremy Symonds,' she replied.

'Your honour?' Lavinia Ramsay looked towards the judge for help.

'Just answer the question, Dr Wainwright,' Judge Cornforth said to the witness. 'It only required a yes or no. We don't need conjecture from you.'

TWO FEET UNDER

The judge was two days away from his seventy fifth birthday and, as the maxim goes, had been around the block a few times. He knew the doctor would ignore his instruction. He had seen her in action before and had a high regard for her.

There were several more questions from the defence lawyer which the pathologist answered. Then...

'Dr Wainwright, what is your relationship with Detective Chief Inspector Cornell?'

There was an intake of breath throughout the court. The judge removed his half-moon spectacles, gave them a brisk clean with a tissue taken from a hand pack, replaced the specs, coughed and prompted the witness.

'Doctor Wainwright?'

Never at any time in her career had Mabel Wainwright been less than confident discussing her subject in court or anywhere else. Now, when her private life had come under scrutiny, she was less self-assured.

'I don't see what that has to do with this case, your honour,' Mabel Wainwright responded, appearing shocked at the question.

'Just answer the question please, doctor,' demanded the defence lawyer.

Wainwright turned towards the judge and took a breath.

'Your honour, I am here to give evidence as to how two females died and to describe the forensics. The defence, as I understand it, can question my evidence, but I am not here to discuss my private life, sir, nor will I.'

'Your honour,' said Lavinia Ramsay, 'it is important to the defence that the jury hears of the relationship between the forensics pathologist and the senior investigating officer in this case.'

'Dr Wainwright?' The judge turned to the witness for further comment.

'Your honour, I am not on trial here and I will not discuss my private life in open court. Not today, not ever. If the court is not happy with my professional competence, it is free to employ someone else.'

Mabel Wainwright sat back in her seat, confidence restored.

As Lavinia Ramsay began to speak, Judge Cornforth intervened.

'I think I know where you are going with this, Mrs Ramsay. If I were to ask the witness whether her relationship with DCI Cornell, whatever that may be, interfered in any way with the direction of this case, would that help?'

'Definitely not, your honour. There are many questions we wish to put to the witness regarding her relationship with the chief inspector,' the defence counsel responded.

'Well, Dr Wainwright has told us,' dictated the judge, 'that she is not going to answer questions about her private life in court and until the defence provides me with evidence that a very respected pathologist has colluded in any way with the senior investigating officer, I am not going to insist that she does. Do you have such evidence?'

'We think that evidence may be exposed during questioning, your honour.'

'Dream on, Mrs Ramsay, dream on. You are not getting away with that,' the judge articulated.

'Would the court note my discontent, your honour?' requested Lavinia Ramsay.

'Noted. Do you have any further questions for this witness, Mrs Ramsay?' the judge asked.

'No, your honour.'

'You are free to step down Doctor Wainwright, and thank you for your meticulous evidence and testimony, as ever. Call your next witness Mr Allardyce.'

The CPS prosecutor called out the name of DCI Max Cornell, who was waiting patiently outside the courtroom.

For the rest of the afternoon both Allardyce and the judge questioned Cornell on the murder investigation including the discovery of the sex ring that had employed the victims.

At the completion of the prosecution's questions, Cornell glanced at the judge, who had a *"what the hell are we doing here?"* look on his face. The hearing was not going the way of the defence, Cornell thought. The judge glanced at his watch.

'I think we'll call it a day. Nine thirty prompt tomorrow for cross examination.'

'All rise,' barked the usher.

They were waiting outside the court, the journalists, reporters, photographers. Mabel had waited for Max and they left together. It had not been the most sensible of decisions.

'*Are you living together? Are you sleeping together? Did you frame Jeremy Symonds?*' were only some of the questions hurled at the couple in rapid succession as they, accompanied by the media throng shoving cameras and microphones into their faces, made their way to their respective vehicles in the court's car park.

Finally able to move on to the road, Max called Mabel on his mobile.

'You are being followed,' Max said.

'Max, I can't handle any of this. Please come to my house.'

'On my way.'

TWO FEET UNDER

Held up by red traffic lights, Max arrived at Mabel's home almost five minutes after she did. Reporters, including those with a TV camera and microphone, surrounded her on the path outside her home. But more of a concern were others who had Marian surrounded a short distance away.

'Back off!' Cornell shouted loud enough for the five reporters surrounding Marian to quieten down. 'You have five seconds to disperse or I'll arrest you for abusing a minor.'

'We were just asking questions, chief inspector,' said one.

'Look guys, you can't go around badgering youngsters and I'm not going to stand here and argue with you. Your five seconds are up. Beat it. Now!'

The reporters stood away. Those surrounding Mabel had now relented, allowing her to grab a frightened Marian and take her inside their home.

'But this is news, chief inspector,' said one of the media crowd.

'You want a good story?' he retorted, 'be in court first thing tomorrow morning.'

There were cries of what, why, when and how, etc. which Cornell ignored. The crowd did not disperse as Cornell went up the path into Mabel's home.

'This has not been a good day,' she said, pulling out a chair for Max to sit at the kitchen table.

'You OK?' Cornell asked Marian who sat opposite.

'Yeah, fine, but it was a bit scary. They get right in your face and ask you so many questions all at once.'

'Tell us about your cross examination, Mabel?' Cornell asked.

While making coffee, the pathologist explained what had taken place in court that morning. Marian was most unhappy at her mother's adversity.

'How can lawyers make up things like that?' she asked.

'Been asking myself the same question for years,' retorted Cornell.

'And what about these journalists? Will they stay all night, Max?' queried Mabel, peering out of the window at the group of reporters and photographers.

'Who knows? They may hang around for a while. Probably be back first thing tomorrow though.'

'Is there a collective noun for journalists?' asked Mabel.

'I think it's a scoop,' said Marian.

'If it isn't, it should be,' said Cornell. 'I imagine there will be a "scoop" of them around my place when I get home.

TWO FEET UNDER

CHAPTER FIVE

There had been no reporters at Cornell's home the previous evening, nor were there any the following morning as Max set out for the crown court. He knew the press would be queuing outside that building already, vying for places to hear his cross examination. He and Mabel had been headlines on both local TV news channels that morning as well as the previous evening. The story of their relationship would still be high profile and there was standing room only in the press area of the court when he arrived.

As Max took his place in the witness box, he noticed his chief superintendent and the chief constable, both expressionless, sitting at the rear of the court trying to appear anonymous.

The first questions from the defence were undertaken by junior counsel and were an unsuccessful attempt to challenge the prosecution's evidence. The young barrister was taking her time learning that if you asked the chief inspector a closed question, you very much got a closed answer in return. Several times during her inquisition the court was left silent as the witness did not qualify his answers beyond yes and no.

Eventually her senior jumped to her feet, her frustration obvious.

'Detective Chief Inspector Cornell,' voiced lead counsel Mrs Lavinia Ramsay, almost shouting, 'what is your relationship with Doctor Mabel Wainwright?'

Max turned to Judge Cornforth.

'You honour if I may? I thought I was here to be cross examined on the evidence I have given with regard to the arrest and the charge of murder against Jeremy Symonds. I am happy to answer other questions along the lines as Mrs Ramsay seeks, but I warn her, she may not like my answers.'

'I can't think for a moment what you could be referring to, chief inspector,' said the judge, but the twinkle in his eye suggested he did. He too had surely heard the rumours regarding the continuing affair of the lead counsel's husband. 'Carry on. Can you remember the question?'

'Yes, your honour.' Cornell cleared his throat. 'Doctor Mabel Wainwright and I are very good friends.'

There was some muted laughter throughout the court.

'How good, chief inspector?' continued Mrs Ramsay.

Cornell paused for a moment, purely for effect. The crowd in the courtroom were on the edge of their seats, waiting for this moment, hoping they would not be disappointed. They weren't.

'Like I said, Doctor Wainwright and I are good friends, but our friendship is probably not as serious as your husband's relationship with the secretary of Eckington Town Council.'

The court erupted. There was some laughter, someone hooted, Cornell distinctly heard one of the younger jurors say, 'get in.' He also noticed his chief superintendent was open mouthed, the chief constable had her head in her hands and the press were hammering away on their tablets and smartphones. The judge, meanwhile, banged his gavel and called several times for order. Mrs Ramsay had sat down and was beginning to look very pale.

The court gradually became quiet.

'Mrs Ramsay,' enquired the judge, 'has the chief inspector answered your question to your satisfaction?'

The lead counsel remained in her seat and did not answer. Her junior, Elizabeth Wakeman, stood hastily in her place at the lectern.

'Your honour, can the defence expect a reason why the witness is not reproached for his answer, and that his answer be struck from the records?'

'Ms Wakeman, if I recall, the chief inspector was asked, quote, "how good?" unquote, his friendship with Dr Wainwright was. By drawing a comparison with another relationship, I thought his answer was quite explicatory. Don't you agree? Carry on.'

'Thank you, your honour. Chief inspector, are you and Doctor Wainwright in an intimate relationship?'

'Can you be a bit more specific?' asked Cornell.

'Do you have intercourse?' the junior barrister said with annoyance.

'Oh yes. We talk all the time,' answered Cornell, resulting in another outbreak of laughter throughout the court, the judge once more banging his gavel for order.

'Counsels for defence and prosecution,' the judge shouted above the clamour, 'my chambers, now! Fifteen minute recess.'

'All rise!' yelled the usher.

Twenty minutes later when everyone had returned to their seats, the judge asked the defence if they wished to address the court.

Elizabeth Wakeman stood. It looked as if Lavinia Ramsay was not going to take any further part in the proceedings.

'Your honour, the defendant wishes to change his plea to guilty.'

'Stand up, Mr Symonds,' demanded Judge Cornforth.

When he had done so, the judge asked, 'do you wish to change your plea?'

'Yes, sir.'

'Has your counsel fully explained the implications of doing so?'

'Yes, sir.'

The judge turned to the witness box.

'You may stand down, Chief Inspector Cornell. The court thanks you for your evidence. Usher, if you would,' the judge directed.

'Jeremy Symonds,' expressed the usher, 'to the charge that on 7th January 2019 you did murder Margaret Whitfield. How do you plead?'

'Guilty.'

The same charge was read out for Sadie Tomkinson with the same pleading.

The judge announced a date when sentencing would take place and thanked everyone for their attendance.

Waiting outside the courtroom were Chief Superintendent Blakeshaw and Chief Constable Mary Dewsbury, together displaying long, miserable faces.

'Morning both,' said Cornell enthusiastically.

'We think you should go home now, Max,' said Chief Superintendent Blakeshaw. 'Take the afternoon off and come and see me in my office first thing tomorrow. Shall we say eight thirty?'

'Any particular reason, sir?'

'Both the chief constable and I feel your answers to the defence lawyers this morning were totally unacceptable for an officer of your standing,' said Blakeshaw.

'Why do you think that, sir?'

'We are not about to discuss it today, chief inspector. We will do so tomorrow. Until then.'

The two senior police officers turned and walked away.

Standing to one side were a few reporters. When Cornell began to walk towards the exit, one stepped forward. There was a camera and a microphone in the background which shot forward to record the conversation.

'Any comment, chief inspector?'

'Yes. Only this; the defence had absolutely no evidence to challenge the prosecution's case, so they tried to manufacture some. They failed.'

'Are you and Doctor Wainwright in a relationship, chief inspector?'

'Not that it makes any difference, but as I said in court, we are good friends. OK?'

'Can we read anything into that, chief inspector?'

'I imagine you will anyway. That's all.'

There were other unobtrusive questions. It flashed through Cornell's mind that he could have told the reporters of his senior officer's disapproval of his court conduct, but decided against it. He had enough to contend with at the moment.

Arriving at his Cullercoats home early afternoon and having collected his dog from next door neighbour Jenny Laidlaw, Max began to explain to Rex what they were going to do that afternoon. Just as he started, his mobile rang.

'Cornell,' he answered.

'Sir, it's Inspector Mary Stewart from Alnwick.'

Mary Stewart had been an inspector south of the Tyne, but had been transferred recently to take over the Alnwick police station, replacing Shaun Lambert who had moved on to Berwick.

'Mary, what can I do for you?'

'Sir, I've got a tricky situation here on a farm north of Alnwick. It's near to a village called East Hewick. I have protesters preventing the farmer from getting his cattle in to milk, sir.'

'Protesters, on a farm!' exclaimed Cornell. 'What the hell are they protesting about?'

'Animal flatulence, sir.'

'I beg your pardon?'

'Animal flatulence,' repeated Stewart. 'Apparently it destroys the ozone layer and contributes to global warming.'

'God give me strength,' retorted Cornell. 'So move them on, Mary. Why do you need me?'

'We've tried, sir, but they superglued themselves to the road when we turned up and I only have two officers with me.'

'I don't believe I'm having this conversation, Mary. So, if they are not harming anything, just leave them be. Walk away.'

'Can't, sir. The farmer says the protesters were here at five o'clock this morning, so the cows have not been milked at all today. He needs to milk them now as they are really suffering. They are Jersey cows, sir, and they are bellowing out in pain. You may be able to hear them in the background. But I'm concerned the protesters may be seriously injured if the cattle are let out of the field and the farmer says he will do that if the protesters are not gone within the hour.'

Cornell could indeed hear the bellowing cattle in the background.

'Is there no other way from the field to his milking sheds?'

'No, sir. The gate is on the corner of the field they are in.'

'Have you told the protestors that if they don't move, a herd of stampeding cattle may trample them to mush?'

TWO FEET UNDER

'Tried that, sir. Their leader, who is a real obnoxious character and hasn't glued himself to the road so he can direct operations, won't listen and just goes on about the world coming to an end. Sir, I'm a bit out of my depth.'

Cornell believed she was near to tears as well.

'Jesus H Christ!' he exclaimed. 'Alright Mary, I'll get to you. Probably take about three quarters of an hour. Can you and the cows hold out till then?'

'I hope so. See you shortly, sir.'

Her voice perked up a little when she knew he was on his way.

The day was sunny and hot, the clouds high. Cornell had changed into jeans and tee shirt. Driving north along the coast to turn off at Blyth and hit the A1 south of Morpeth, his dog was sitting next to him and looking every inch a passenger with the seat belt across his chest.

Cornell wondered if he would be suspended for what he had said in court that morning. The chief constable would certainly not be happy and there was no doubt she would be answering reporters' questions at this very moment about his remarks.

Cornell never could help himself. He blamed his mother. She had always told him never to accept being talked down to. He may not be better than anyone else, she had said, but he was just as good.

Cornell took that on board at an early age and was in trouble with teachers throughout his schooldays, then with his superiors in the police force.

Being tall didn't help. He often found himself "volunteering" for things he wasn't interested in, or being labelled as the main troublemaker when a misdemeanour was committed. He recalled an incident when his Protestant school was having a snowball fight with the Catholic school, like you do, across the road which divided the two establishments. The battle was well underway when the local dustbin lorry, determined to get through at all costs, came between the two factions. Cornell could still hear the drumming noise as two hundred handmade, half frozen missiles peppered the vehicle, some finding their way into the cab.

The complaint and the resultant investigation pointed the finger at Cornell. His argument that he was not the only one present and had not organised the fight, which was an annual event, were in vain. He took his caning of four of the best like a man, with a smile on his face, which troubled the headmaster for days after.

Cornell's mobile rang. It was Doctor Mabel Wainwright.

'I've heard Symonds changed his plea to guilty, Max. What prompted that?' she asked.

'The judge asked the barristers to see him in chambers and when they came back, Symonds changed his plea.'

'But why? Did the defence ask you about us?'

'Oh, yes. I said we were in a relationship but it probably wasn't as serious as Mrs Ramsay's husband's with the clerk of Ecklington Council.'

'Oh my God, Max! You didn't!'

'Did.'

'What happened then?' Mabel asked anxiously.

'Got the impression the judge knew all about Mr Ramsay's extra curriculum activity and enjoyed the fact I'd highlighted it in court. It was then the defence must have realised their attempts to smear you and me was beginning to bite them in the arse. They had nothing left to argue with and therefore no option but to change their plea.'

'Where are you now?' Doctor Wainwright asked.

'I'm currently on the road heading north to meet some people protesting about farting cattle.'

There was a silence. 'You still there, Mabel?' Cornell asked.

'Farting cattle? Max are you ever serious?' she asked, trying not to laugh.

'Always. These are Jersey cattle by all accounts, destroying the ozone layer, the buggers. The protesters are preventing them from being milked. By the way, what's the best stuff to remove superglue? They have glued themselves to the road.'

'Acetone.'

'Where can I get that?' asked Cornell.

'Chemist, hardware stores. Probably the latter as you will need a quantity of it. Or the farm itself. If it's dairy they may have some for cleaning purposes.'

'Right. Anything else?'

'Yes. Marian is staying over at a friend's tomorrow night. Why don't you come over? I'll make dinner for us and I'll slaughter a buffalo for your dog.'

'He heard that. He's offended.'

'You have him with you?'

'Yeah. He needs some fresh air. Love for us both to come tomorrow night, Mabel. Must go now as I'm approaching this farm of farting cattle. I can hear them already. Not in tune either.'

'Methane produced by farm animals is a major contributor to global warming. We must reduce the………'

'Sir, I don't really care about that at the moment,' Cornell responded.

'Well you should. By the year…….'

'What is your name?' demanded Cornell of the protest leader, who as Mary Stewart had warned, appeared somewhat arrogant.

'Councillor James Dickinson.'

'And why are you here, Mr Dickinson?'
'It's councillor.'
'OK, Councillor Dickinson, why are you here?'
And off went Councillor Dickinson on a diatribe of global disasters that had and were about to befall the human race.

Meanwhile the farmer arrived in a Range Rover. Both rear windows were open and two sheep dogs barked out of each when they saw Rex, who was sniffing around the protestors, prostrate in various positions on the road. He ignored the barking dogs.

'Time is up,' shouted the farmer as he got out of his vehicle. 'I can't wait any longer. Those cows have to be milked and they have to be milked now. Who are you?' he asked Cornell, whose first thought was that the man was dressed rather well for a farmer.

'I'm DCI Max Cornell,' said Max displaying his ID.

'Good. I'm glad you are here. Get these bloody people off my land.'

'Can I have your name, sir?' requested Cornell.

'Didn't you hear me? Get these people moved. Now!'

The farmer grabbed Max's arm to emphasise his instruction.

Max in turn grabbed the farmer's arm and squeezed hard.

'You are hurting my arm,' the farmer whined.

'And you are seriously testing my patience. Now what's your name?' Max shouted the question in the farmer's face.

'Joseph Henry Lockheed. I am the farmer here.'

'Right, Mr Lockheed,' Max let loose of his arm and shouting to be heard above the sound of the barking dogs, asked, 'have you any acetone on the farm so we can get this lot moved?'

'We use it on the farm to clean instruments,' the farmer shouted back, rubbing his forearm.

'Great. Go get some.'

Lockheed looked aggrieved at having been spoken to in that manner, but took out his mobile and requested someone at the farm bring some acetone to the incident, at the double.

Meanwhile, Dickinson was still banging on to Inspector Mary Stewart about the evils of farming and how we have to change our diets and get rid of all farm animals. Stewart's attempts at putting forward rational explanations for not doing so, were emphatically ignored.

'Inspector Stewart,' hollered DCI Cornell, 'caution that man that if he doesn't shut up we will arrest him for animal cruelty and obstructing the police.'

'Yes, sir,' replied the inspector. She instructed a constable to administer the caution while looking at Cornell quizzically. Those charges wouldn't stick, her face depicted. Cornell merely shrugged.

Cornell looked around; the farm was some hundred metres to his left with hills in the background. To his right was the village of East Hewick, the church tower and spire prominent above the red roofs of the houses. It would have been a pleasant vision had it not been for a cacophony of barking dogs, bellowing cattle and a farmer shouting at protesters whose leader was shouting back.

A quad bike arrived driven by a young man carrying a five litre plastic carton of acetone. Within minutes with farmers and police working together, the seven protestors were released. However, outnumbering their adversaries, they continued to lie on the road and tried to re-glue themselves.

'Mr Lockheed,' ordered Cornell, 'get your cows moving now before this lot get a chance to glue themselves again.'

Lockheed spoke to his farmhand who drove off on his quad bike in the direction of the bellowing cattle.

'I would get out off the road, chief inspector, they will come fast,' advised the farmer, no longer exasperated at the situation which was now improving.

Lockheed got into his vehicle, did an impressive three point turn and drove off in the direction of the farm.

Five minutes later the group of protestors forgot about refastening themselves to the road and hurriedly stood up, only just making it to the safety of the fence as a mass of clamouring Jersey cows bore down on them. Cornell held Rex beside him at the side of the road to avoid him being caught up in the stampede.

When the herd had passed, the road was covered with a mixture of milk, urine and shit, and Cornell, sure that the protestors no longer had the enthusiasm for lying amongst it, suggested they all go home.

Dickinson continued delivering his sermon however, despite his followers leaving, picking their way carefully along the road.

'Don't you ever take a breath, sir?' asked Cornell.

'How dare you! I am going to report you and will take this up with my MP. You have no right to stop me from protesting. It is my right as a British subject. I am trying to save the planet from destruction and you…..'

Cornell wandered far enough away to be out of earshot. On her request, he advised Mary Stewart how to write the incident up, offering an addendum if she required it.

'But I'm betting that we have not heard the last of James Dickinson,' Cornell said as he and his dog returned to their vehicle.

CHAPTER SIX

'So, chief inspector, do you think your answer to the defence counsel's question was appropriate for a police officer of your rank?' asked Chief Superintendent Blakeshaw at eight thirty the following morning, after taking a sip of coffee.

The two officers were once again sitting in the chief superintendent's office, Cornell not having been asked if he would like coffee. This didn't really bother him, although its smell suggested it was of better quality than that of his superior's predecessor.

'One thing I have a problem with, sir, is solicitors and barristers fabricating situations and stories to defend their guilty clients. We had Symonds DNA on both victims, his footprint at one of the scenes and he fit the profile one hundred percent. He should have pleaded guilty, but the defence thought they could embarrass Doctor Wainwright and myself, then imply that our relationship could have prejudiced the case. In the circumstances my answer was certainly not inappropriate, sir.'

'But you accused the husband of an eminent law officer of having an affair.'

'I didn't accuse him, sir, I stated a fact. And he's no longer having an affair. It's now a long term extra marital relationship.'

'And you know this, how?'

'Doctor Wainwright told me.'

Superintendent Blakeshaw blinked at his chief inspector with astonishment.

'But....how does she know? She could have been making it up. What if it isn't true?'

'Doctor Wainwright doesn't make things up, sir.'

'The chief constable has told me to discipline you.'

'What for, sir?'

The chief superintendent was exasperated and concerned. Exasperated for the audacity of his chief inspector and concerned for the inadequacy he felt in his company.

'I'm not sure myself now,' was all he could say on that matter. 'However,' he continued, 'there is something else. We received a complaint from a member of the public yesterday afternoon regarding your conduct. This is especially serious as you were not supposed to be on duty yesterday afternoon. The complainant is a Councillor Dickinson, who claims you unlawfully prevented him and others from legal protesting and were verbally abusive towards him.'

Cornell described the previous afternoon's demonstration at the farm and his successful solution.

'The man is a lunatic, sir, who I find hard to believe is a councillor.'

'Shouldn't Inspector Stewart have been able to handle this situation herself? Did she have to call on you?'

'In another world, sir, perhaps. But the current policing policies do not allow you to use your imagination. Today, sir, the perpetrator's human rights are at the forefront of policing and young officers like Mary Stewart don't know how to cope with situations like protests, other than to stand back and let them take their course.'

'And,' interjected Chief Superintendent Blakeshaw, 'unlike Inspector Mary Stewart, a conscientious officer who takes great care not to offend anyone, DCI Cornell doesn't care who he offends. Have I got that right, chief inspector?'

'Stretching it a bit, sir, but I did stop the protest, the farmer got his cattle in for milking and no one, including the animals, were hurt and I learned animal flatulence destroys the ozone layer and acetone removes superglue. A good result, I would have thought.'

Cornell was excused and he returned to his office. He had no current murders to solve, only two stabbings, an armed robbery and several serious assault incidents, one of which could end up being a murder. Near midday, his mobile rang. The caller was Inspector Mary Stewart.

'Yes, Mary. More protests?'

'Sir, I've got a body. That place we were at yesterday, East Hewick.'

'What, on that farm?'

'No, sir. In the village. In the graveyard of St Peter's Church of England. Sir, it's Councillor Dickinson. The man who......'

'Shit, I knew we'd not seen the last of him,' Cornell interrupted, 'but I didn't expect him to turn up dead, and so soon. Pathologist been called, Mary?'

'Yes, sir. First call as per your instructions. It's Doctor Mabel Wainwright. She is on her way.'

'Fine. Do what you have to, to preserve the crime scene. I'll be there as soon as I can.'

Cornell took Marty Fielding and Irene Stainton with him. The weather was warm but a slight drizzle kept the windscreen wipers working intermittently.

Several onlookers dressed in mackintoshes and anoraks had congregated at the scene. *Ghoulish or curious?* The pathologist's tent had been hastily erected over the body and tape was secured around a number of gravestones to form a square.

Inspector Mary Stewart and two of her officers stood outside this area awaiting instructions from Cornell.

Tom Mawson, Wainwright's assistant, was dressed in waterproofs and was on his hands and knees within the confines of the tape searching in the grass between the gravestones, looking for anything that pertained to the incident.

Cornell knew better than to ask a pathologist questions so soon after arrival. He joined Mary Stewart and the other officers.

'What time was the body discovered, Inspector,' he asked, 'and who found it?'

'The body was discovered at half past nine this morning, sir, by the man who cuts the grass. His name is Dennis Percival. He's very upset and is currently in the church being consoled by the vicar.'

'He cuts grass in the rain?' asked Cornell.

'Those modern lawnmowers can cope with the wet, sir,' said DC Fielding, 'although it leaves a hell of a mess.'

Cornell looked around and observed a seat mounted lawnmower parked off to one side and that the grass behind it had been cut. The graveyard appeared to be well maintained.

'Possible suspect?' he asked.

'I doubt it, sir,' the inspector replied. 'He is little more than a boy and appears really shaken up. If he is involved, he's a very good actor.'

'Did he report the find himself, or to somebody else?'

'Percival went to the shop across the street, sir. The owner, her name is Gladys Hume, came over here first to check he was telling the truth, then she dialled 999.'

'Is she one of those stood over there?' Cornell pointed towards the bystanders milling around by the lich gate.

'No, sir. I imagine she will be in her shop.'

'And you are sure it's James Dickinson lying over there in the tent, Mary?'

'Yes, sir. No question.'

'OK. Go and see Percival in the church and see if he's up to making a statement. Marty and Irene, do a door-to-door in the immediate vicinity. Find out if anyone knew Dickinson and saw him or anyone else here last night or early this morning.'

Cornell turned to one of the Alnwick police officers. 'PC Green, isn't it? I remember you from the Symonds investigation. Have a look around the graveyard and see if you can find what Dickinson was doing here.'

As the group dispersed, Cornell walked over to the tent and opened the flap.

'Good morning, doctor. How are you today?'

Mabel Wainwright, devoid of makeup and her blonde hair tied in a severe ponytail rendering her less attractive than she would normally appear, pulled her one size fits all paper overall straight and turned towards Cornell.

'Morning, Max. Multiple stab wounds to the chest and abdomen, most likely with a knife. Probably died from blood loss although I suspect one laceration may have entered the heart. Dead for at least twelve hours and Tom thinks he may have been killed somewhere else and brought here.'

'How does he know that?'

'No sign of a struggle here and he would have struggled.'

'Anything else? Perpetrator right handed or left?'

'Not sure. I think the victim may have been stabbed by someone standing behind him. In which case, from the position of the wounds, the perpetrator would probably be left handed. Likely to be a man, but I suppose it could be a woman. The deceased is not a big man.'

'His name is James Dickinson. He was the leader of yesterday's anti-flatulence movement at the nearby farm.'

'That's interesting. The farmer will be in the frame, then?'

'Yes, but I want to do a bit of digging around the village first before I start accusing anybody.'

TWO FEET UNDER

Mabel Wainwright smiled as he left her, thinking of their date for that evening and hoping he would make it.

CHAPTER SEVEN

Leaving the scene supervision to the other Alnwick police officer, Cornell walked across the street to the village shop. The sign above the window advertised it as a general dealer and post office. A poster on the glass door promoted the national lottery.

Cornell looked along the road through the centre of this quiet village, which couldn't be described as anything other than picturesque. There were houses on either side of the road, those he could see into had attractive gardens. Some houses were semi-detached and there was a terrace of six bungalows that looked like pensioners homes. A road to the left went into what looked like a council housing estate. He could see a pub sign in the distance and two bus stops almost opposite each other. Two people stood waiting at one. Several residents, ignoring the damp, were in their gardens looking in his direction.

Cornell opened the door of the shop and a bell jangled above his head startling him. A man was serving an elderly woman at the post office window while a plump, middle aged woman and a teenage girl were serving groceries and vegetables to several customers. Cornell stood in the small queue to await his turn. He would have described the interior of the shop as old fashioned, something perhaps from the fifties. It was not well lit and smelt of vegetables and old age.

'What can I do for you?' asked the woman, most politely.

Cornell produced his warrant card ID.

'I'm DCI Max Cornell. You called emergency services this morning to report a body in the graveyard?'

It was a question rather than a statement. The lady's face took on a serious look.

'You mean the murder? Yes, that was me. I didn't find the body though,' the lady stressed emphatically, 'that was young Dennis Percival. He cuts the grass in the church yard. It's James Dickinson, isn't it? The body, I mean.'

'Did you know him, Mrs Hume?'

'Of course I did. Everybody in the village knew James Dickinson.'

'You mentioned murder, Mrs Hume. Why do you think he was murdered?'

'I just assumed he had been. Why are you lot here? You wouldn't be here doing house to house enquiries if he'd died of a heart attack, would you?'

The lady had a point.

'Do you know of anyone who would want to hurt Mr Dickinson or want him dead?'

'Just about everybody in the village.'
'Why do you say that, Mrs Hume?'
'Because nobody liked him.'

Cornell felt as if he were pulling teeth.

'And why did nobody like him, Mrs Hume?'

'Because he was a self-righteous bastard who interfered with everyone and everything and was critical of anyone who didn't follow his ridiculous conspiracy theories.'

'Did you see Mr Dickinson or anyone else around the graveyard last night?'

'No. Should I?'

After a few more questions, Cornell felt he had come to the end of this fact finding mission. The only thing he had learned from Gladys Hume was James Dickinson's address, the only piece of information the aggressive shopkeeper had divulged willingly.

'Thank you, Mrs Hume. That's all for now, but I may have to come back to see you again.'

Cornell left the shop, the bell above the door jangling again as he left. He spotted DC's Fielding and Stainton talking with the Alnwick officers across the road and went to talk to them.

'Anything?' he asked.

'Not a thing, sir,' reported Fielding. 'We've done half a dozen houses. Nobody saw anything or heard anything. Everyone seems to have known

TWO FEET UNDER

Dickinson and most of the people I've spoken to are pleased he's dead.'

'That's nice. And you, Irene?'

'More of the same, sir. Dickinson was certainly not well liked and one guy told me that it was only a matter of time before somebody did him in.'

'Bloody hell,' exclaimed Cornell. 'So, we are not short of suspects, then.'

He looked at his watch. It was almost two thirty. He felt a pang of hunger.

'You find anything?' Cornell asked PC Green who joined them after his sojourn around the graveyard.

'Only found a bunch of flowers up against the wall. Seem to have been thrown there, which is strange because they are still reasonably fresh. Could have been blown, I suppose, but I don't recall there being much wind lately. Not sure if they are important or if we can get anything off them, but I bagged them anyway.'

'Good man. Give the bag to Tom Mawson.'

The officers returned to the crime scene just in time to see the coroner's van drive off with the body of James Dickinson in the back. Mabel Wainwright and Tom Mawson, assisted by the police officer from Alnwick, were packing up. PC Green went to help shake the dampness from the tarpaulin.

'So, what's the score, doctor?' asked Cornell, keeping their relationship on a professional basis in front of colleagues.

'Stabbed at least five times, chief inspector, by a knife blade that is about an inch wide. Don't know how long until I open him up, but very sharp. And Tom found something too. Tom, over here.'

Tom Mawson left the packing of equipment and walked over to the pair. He took a polythene bag out of his overall pocket.

'I found this under the body, chief inspector.'

Mawson held the bag and Cornell had to look hard to find what was being displayed. There, in one corner was a small silver coloured object.

'I see it, but what the hell is it?'

'I think it's a link from a silver alloy watch strap, chief inspector, perhaps from a watch damaged in the attack. Dickinson's watch was still on him intact, so it could be the perpetrator's.'

'So, the murderer could be minus a watch?'

'Could be, chief inspector,' said Mawson. 'I've looked all around the crime scene and can't find anything else of importance. There are marks on the grass left by footwear but are not suggestive of a struggle and insufficient for taking impressions. There is a little blood, but less than I would expect at a murder scene.'

'Which strengthens the argument he was killed elsewhere. Thanks, Tom.'

'Must get back to Newcastle,' said Doctor Wainwright suddenly. 'I have a friend coming for dinner tonight.'

'Yeah. I hope he makes it. Catch you later, doctor,' returned Cornell, hoping he could keep the dinner date and that no one within earshot picked up on the fact he knew the gender of the doctor's guest.

CHAPTER EIGHT

Gladys Hume followed the chief inspector to the shop door and watched him walk across the wet road to talk to a group of people, no doubt his colleagues as some were in uniform. Gladys stood aside to allow the last of the current customers to leave the shop.

The tall policeman who had asked her questions concerned her. He smiled the whole time he was asking. It unsettled her. He didn't appear to be serious.

'What did you tell him?' asked the man behind the post office grille.

'What do you think? Nothing,' she retorted angrily.

'They are sure to find something.'

'Not if we all keep our mouths shut, you idiot.'

'Somebody's bound to say something,' the man challenged.

'Well, it had better not be you.'

The landline in the shop rang. Gladys didn't have a mobile. The man picked the receiver up and answered.

'Yes, he's gone,' and after a pause, 'no, I didn't speak to him. Here,' offering the phone to Gladys.

TWO FEET UNDER

'What?' she said and after listening to the caller for a few seconds, 'I didn't say anything. Look, it's you who got us into this mess. Don't go interrogating me when something you've done makes it worse.'

Gladys held the phone listening to the caller for a few more seconds.

'Then you better hope he keeps his mouth shut as well,' and with that comment Gladys slammed the phone down.

'I'm going for a break,' said the man behind the grille.

Gladys turned to the assistant who was standing by the till. The young woman had heard the communication. She had heard similar communications before. She knew there was something wrong in the village, but didn't know what it was. She knew her employer was involved but didn't dare ask. Gladys had a temper, and there weren't many jobs around East Hewick where you could fall out of bed into one.

'You go for your break as well,' Gladys informed the assistant. 'I'll look after things.'

Gladys Hume had lived all her life in the village. Her parents ran the post office cum general dealers before her and she was left the business when they retired. Both now dead, Gladys wondered how her mother and father would have coped with the trouble.

CHAPTER NINE

The church interior was cool and dark, like every other Protestant church Cornell had ever been in. Cornell heard Inspector Stewart, the vicar and Dennis Percival talking quietly before he saw them. Once his eyes became acclimatised to the low light, he followed the direction of grass blemished footprints on the floor of the church to the pews where they were sitting.

Percival, young enough to have just left school, wore a light weight anorak, a pale green tee shirt and khaki shorts. His mousy coloured hair was long and damp, tied in a pony tail and he sported a meagre beard in a vain attempt to cover his acne. He did, however, appear relatively composed as Mary Stewart introduced the chief inspector to the Reverend Neville Mason, a small, thin, wiry man, dressed in grey flannels and a striped shirt, open at the neck displaying his dog collar.

'How is Dennis?' asked Cornell.

'OK,' said Mary Stewart, placing a written document inside a folder. 'He's given us a statement.'

'Fine. He can go back to work now. Everything is cleared up in the graveyard.'

'I'd rather go home if you don't mind,' Percival stated.

'That's OK, too,' Cornell agreed. The young man, barely more than a boy with little flesh attached to his frame, looked relieved. He picked up his beanie hat and began to walk towards the church exit.

'But you must come back later and finish cutting the grass, Dennis,' said the vicar.

Not very Christian; the lad must have had a fright finding a body.

'Reverend, did you know the deceased?' asked Cornell.

'Yes, I think everyone in the village knew James.'

'Was he a churchgoer?'

'Yes, yes, he was,' answered the vicar.

'Did you know him well? You referred to him by his first name.'

'I try to call all my flock by their Christian names if I can remember them, but James rarely missed church on a Sunday.'

'Do you know why he was in the graveyard last night?'

'No, I'm afraid not.'

'Did he go to the graveyard often?'

'Not to my knowledge,' the vicar replied.

'Do you know of anyone who would want to harm James?'

'No, I do not.'

'Mrs Hume in the shop told me James was badly liked.'

'I'm afraid I do not get involved with people's popularity. There is a bit of good in everyone and that was how I saw James.'

'What is going on here?' asked a voice from the direction of the church door.

A tall woman stood by the font. She wore a straw hat and was dressed in overalls covering a rugby shirt. Gloves were sticking out of a rear pocket. She was damp from the drizzle.

'Ah, this is my wife, Mavis,' the vicar said getting to his feet. 'These are police officers, dear. Are we finished, chief inspector?'

'Is Mrs Mason aware of the body found in the graveyard?' asked Cornell.

'Of course,' the vicar's wife answered. 'It's James Dickinson, isn't it?'

'Mrs Mason,' Cornell got to his feet and walked over to where the vicar's wife was standing, 'when was the last time you saw James Dickinson?'

'It would have been last Sunday at Evensong.'

'How did he seem?'

'Same as always.'

'Do you know of anyone who would wish him harm, Mrs Mason?'

'Just about everyone in the whole village,' the vicar's wife responded. 'I'm afraid James upset people.'

'Do you have any idea why he would be in the graveyard yesterday evening?'

'I have no idea,' Mavis Mason responded.

'We wouldn't have known he was there, would we?' added Reverend Mason.

'Did James have a partner, or is there any other close relative who needs to be informed of his death?'

'I don't know, chief inspector,' replied the vicar. 'He was married once, but got divorced a while ago. He had a son, but he died.'

'OK,' said Cornell. 'We will leave it there for the moment. Thank you Reverend and Mrs Mason. I've no doubt we'll speak again.'

Cornell almost laughed as he and Mary Stewart left the church. Much like the shopkeeper Mrs Hume, the vicar and his wife hadn't offered any useful information at all. Both may as well have said "no comment," for all the data they had provided.

'I'm starving,' said Cornell when he and Mary Stewart met up with the other officers. 'Let's go and see if that pub does meals.'

The six police men and women walked off towards the *Sword and Lance;* Cornell entered first.

TWO FEET UNDER

The bar was almost empty save for two elderly men playing dominoes in a corner of the room. A man stood behind the bar polishing glasses.

'Hi!' the man barked enthusiastically. 'I'm Bill Walton. Welcome to my humble pub.'

The man, jovial no doubt, because he saw his afternoon's takings increasing substantially. 'You will be here about the murder then.'

'You know about it already?' queried Cornell.

'Yes, just been to the shop. It will be all around the village by now.'

'Did you know James Dickinson?'

'Unfortunately, yes. I had to bar him from the pub. He was chasing away my customers. A pub is not the place to promote conspiracy theories. I mean, some are worth looking at, but you'll never convince me Princess Diana's death was caused by Prince Philip on a motorbike. Actually, I felt sorry for him, Dickinson that is, being hated and living all by himself.'

'He was married once, as it happens.'

'Don't tell me. She left.'

'Looks like it. Do you do meals, by the way?'

'Not until six, but I can knock together some sandwiches if you can wait ten minutes. Egg and tomato or chicken OK?' the barman added.

'That's fine,' answered Cornell for everyone.

'Drinks?' asked Walton.

Irene Stainton agreed to act as drinks waiter.

After serving the drinks the barman went through a door to the kitchen. The two men playing dominoes were engrossed in their game and had barely looked up when the police had entered the building.

'So, we have a body,' said Cornell quietly, so his voice would not be heard by the domino contestants. 'A frantic stabbing. Tom Mawson thinks Dickinson was probably killed elsewhere and dumped in the graveyard. No blood trails, no pronounced footmarks. We know the identity of the deceased and his address and have part of a watch strap, possibly belonging to the killer. However, the residents we've spoken to so far are not very cooperative, in fact they are positively obstructive.'

The barman walked in with a tray of sandwiches.

'These are yesterday's, but they've been in the cooler all night and still look good to me. Couldn't help hearing that last remark. I'm afraid you will not get much cooperation from the residents of this village, chief inspector.'

'You the owner of this establishment, sir?' Cornell asked.

'Tenant. Been here just over a year. Spent twelve years on the rigs before that, the reason for my divorce. However, I made a fortune and moved here believing it to be a quaint, picturesque village nestling in the foothills of the Cheviots, where a man could hang up his guns, so to speak.'

'And it's not?' asked Cornell.

'It is the most miserable place on earth. The most exciting it ever gets is when the winner of the village hall domino card draw is announced at the Saturday night dance. I'm an outsider here and I probably always will be. I'm tolerated because I run the pub. I barely make a living, but it's home, at least for the time being. I'm contemplating joining a monastery to find exhilaration.'

'Do you work here all by yourself?' queried Irene Stainton, smiling at the tenant's humour.

'Most of the time. One of the villagers works for me part time.'

'Any reason for the natives to be so disobliging?' enquired Fielding.

'I have yet to discover that,' answered the host. 'There are many possible scenarios. I've heard several across the bar, one concerns the farm.'

'Do you mean the Lockheed farm?' ventured Cornell.

'Yes. You have heard the rumours tóo?'

'No. Inspector Stewart and I were there yesterday sorting out some protesters.'

'Ah! Yes, James Dickinson and his merry band of activists. I wonder what will happen to them now he's dead. It's strange none of them lived in the village. You met Joseph Lockheed, the farmer?'

'We did.'

'I don't know what it is, but there is some history between the Lockheed family and this village. Some dark history. I don't know what, but the name Lockheed is mentioned in whispered undertones.'

'That's a bit dramatic, isn't it?' questioned Irene Stainton.

'I wouldn't be surprised if Lockheed is the number one suspect for Dickinson's murder on the current grapevine of whispered undertones.'

Walton retreated behind the bar and the team ate their sandwiches. Cornell liked the tenant of the pub. His dry sense of humour was similar to his own.

The two men in the corner had now decided to leave, conducting a post-mortem on their last game of dominos as they left, via a visit to the gents.

'Not too bad,' said Fielding about the sandwiches, 'considering they're a day old. Is this farmer, Lockheed, our chief suspect, sir?'

'I suppose he should be, but I'm not convinced.'

'Why is that, sir?' asked Stainton.

'He wouldn't have had time to milk his cows, plan a murder and know where Dickinson would be to carry it out. I could be wrong of course, he could have planned the murder before the protest. There may be a lot more to it. I'll go and see him now. Marty, with me.'

'Anything I can do before I go back to Alnwick?' asked Mary Stewart.

'Yes, Mary. Would you and your officers gain entry into Dickinson's home and do a top to bottom search. I'll call in at Alnwick tomorrow morning on my way back here. Irene, back to the station now. Bring Sergeant Donaldson up to date and get everything we know on to the whiteboard.'

CHAPTER TEN

Cornell and Fielding drove to the farm on the same road the protesters had blocked the day before. The farm was in a valley, with fields of varying types of crops stretching far into the distance. They entered a neat and tidy farmyard, the buildings and yard shiny from the rain. Lockheed's Range Rover was parked in front of the farmhouse and Cornell parked next to it.

The house was big, three storeys no less, with two entrance doors side by side. The left one was open and Lockheed appeared through it as the two officers were closing their car doors. The man stopped in his tracks, looking surprised.

'Morning, Mr Lockheed,' said Cornell, estimating the farmer would be in his early forties.

'Good morning, chief inspector. Are you here on police business?'

'Yes, we are. Have you heard that James Dickinson is dead, Mr Lockheed? We are treating his death as suspicious.'

'Bloody hell. No. I haven't. Well I never. Can't say I'm too upset though.'

'I can understand that, Mr Lockheed. Could we have a chat inside?'

'I suppose so. Come on in out of the wet. I suppose I'll be the number one suspect?'

Cornell followed the farmer through the open door into a spacious stone floored utility room. There was a huge table in the middle of the floor, three upright freezers against the walls, two large sinks and shelves containing tins and packages of all shapes and sizes. At the table sat two women, one much older than Lockheed, the other about his age and a girl of three or four. They were packing trays of eggs.

'James Dickinson is dead,' Lockheed announced to the two women, who looked at each other, surprise on both their faces. 'Mother, this is chief inspector err....' Lockheed looked round at his visitors.

'Cornell, and this is DC Fielding,' returned the senior police officer.

'This is my mother Edna Lockheed, my wife Eleanor and my granddaughter, Jennifer.'

'Pleased to meet you, ladies and Jennifer.'

The little girl got up and hid her face in the clothes of the elder woman.

'Sit down, both of you.' Edna Lockheed pointed to two chairs while asking the girl to retake her seat, which she did. 'I'll make tea. How did Dickinson die?'

'He was found dead in the graveyard this morning. We think he was murdered,' explained

Fielding, adding, 'although we can't divulge how he met his death at this stage.'

'Am I a suspect?' Lockheed asked again.

Cornell looked at the farmer's hands. He was wearing a watch with a leather strap on his left wrist.

'Can you account for your whereabouts between when I left here yesterday afternoon and this morning?' asked Cornell.

'I was with two of the lads milking until late as there was almost twice the normal output. Then we had to can it to be ready for collection this morning. I didn't get to the house until after midnight. I had a bite to eat, cup of coffee, shower, then got to bed around one. My wife will vouch for that because I woke her up.'

Eleanor Lockheed nodded her assent.

'Do you have another watch, Mr Lockheed?'

'No, just this one. Had it years, never lost a second. It's on its third strap. Why do you ask?'

'It's nothing. I met the landlord of the village pub earlier today, Bill Walton. He said your family had some history with the village. Do you know what he meant?'

Lockheed sat down and gave a huge sigh.

'Still going on about that after all these years,' he said.

'About what, Mr Lockheed? Enlighten me.'

TWO FEET UNDER

Mrs Lockheed placed enormous cups on the table and a plastic beaker of orange juice for the girl. The older woman poured hot water from an old kettle into a large tea pot and stirred it, then carried it with milk from a fridge and sugar from a cupboard to the table.

The little girl seemed lost in a world of her own, determinedly colouring an elephant in a children's book with a purple crayon.

'I'll put you in the picture, chief inspector,' Edna Lockheed announced, pouring tea for the adults. 'East Hewick used to be a lovely place. But during the sixties and early seventies, a number of posh people moved here as the houses were big, but cheap. One was a retired judge called Dickinson who thought he had a mandate to control the village. Cliques were created, those who followed the judge and those who didn't and others that didn't care, and it caused problems.

'On the farm we were shielded from the conflict to some extent, but couldn't help but become involved when our Joseph here, got his girlfriend pregnant. She was called Stephanie Woods and was only sixteen, the same age as him. Her parents, backed by the previous vicar and the church wardens, insisted they get married, and despite my and his father's concerns, they did. It was a huge mistake. Stephanie was not cut out to be a farmer's wife. Collecting eggs and mucking out cow byers was definitely not her scene.'

Cornell shuffled in his seat, wondering where this was going. Edna Lockheed noticed.

'Be patient, chief inspector, I'm getting there. Joseph and Stephanie had twins, yes, twin girls were born, but Stephanie only gave it four or five months then moved back in with her parents. Then after maybe a couple of months more, she left the village, the area. It broke her parents hearts, particularly her father who idolised her. They separated about two years later and he left the village. Her mother stayed in East Hewick for a while, but couldn't handle the gossip. She eventually left and moved to Berwick. I heard she died about six or seven years ago. The police did trace Stephanie at the time and came to tell us, as she and Joseph were still married, but they wouldn't reveal her whereabouts.'

'It took me ages to convince the court I didn't have her address to serve divorce papers,' said Joseph Lockheed.

'So, what became of the twins?' asked Cornell, sufficiently interested to follow the story through, but not yet knowing of its relevance.

'I brought them up with the help of my mother,' replied Lockheed. 'The twins and Eleanor and I, got married on the same day five years ago. Lesley to one of our farm hands and Wendy to another village lad, Peter Dickinson. Wendy and Peter also had twins, which is not unusual if a parent is a twin.'

Edna Lockheed's expression took on a sombre look before continuing with the narrative.

'Then about four months ago, Wendy, Peter and one of their children, their son, Hugh, were killed in a car crash on the A1. The other child, Jennifer, survived and this is she,' she said, putting her hand on the girl's shoulder.

'I recall the incident,' said Cornell trying to remain polite. Fascinating as the story was, he hoped the conclusion was not far away.

'Chief inspector, the father of Wendy's husband, Peter, is, or was, I should say, James Dickinson, the protester, the man who was found dead in the graveyard this morning.'

'So, Jennifer here is granddaughter of both Joseph and James Dickinson. Are you saying there was more to James Dickinson's protestations?'

'Yes, chief inspector,' declared Eleanor. 'James Dickinson wanted custody of Jennifer and had made threats of court action.'

'On what grounds? That he was her grandfather?'

'Yes. The papers had not been served, but we received a letter from his solicitors that they were going to be. The grounds were that the farm was too dangerous for an infant, that we were all too busy to look after her properly and that he, Dickinson, as a householder with no ties, was much better equipped to look after her.'

'I'm not an expert in children's law,' expressed Cornell, 'but I'm not sure a court would grant custody to a single man over a family, unless there was something radically wrong with the family.'

'The protest the other day, and other protests before that,' explained Lockheed, 'were not about climate change, it was just to cause us more aggravation.'

'Why would he do that?' asked Cornell.

'Because I got the girl, chief inspector.'

'I think you had better explain, Mr Lockheed.'

Joseph Lockheed poured himself another cup of tea.

'Twenty seven years ago, Stephanie Woods was a happy-go-lucky girl. She was really popular in the village with children and adults alike. A real darling and absolutely gorgeous. I was infatuated with her at school, as were most of the boys in our class who were insanely jealous of me going out with her. When her pregnancy became known, there are those in the village who said I must have raped her and when she left the village, they said it was because I had abused her. It has been held against me ever since.'

'So you are not invited to open the annual village fête then?' joked Cornell. He continued. 'Councillor James Dickinson doesn't seem to have been all that popular either.'

'He wasn't a councillor,' said Edna Lockheed. 'He had been a parish councillor once, for a few months, but he created so much trouble, all the other councillors resigned. There was a council election and he stood, but nobody voted for him this time. He claimed the election was rigged and called himself councillor ever since.'

'He was never popular,' continued Joseph Lockheed. 'We were in the same class at school.'

'Was he infatuated with Stephanie Woods too?'

'Oh, yes. Absolutely. More than anybody. More than me. He kept asking her out, wouldn't take no for an answer.'

'What did Stephanie think of him?' asked Cornell.

'She enjoyed the attention, while at the same time she thought he was pathetic.'

'How did he react to you?'

'Oh, he really hated me with a vengeance.'

'Did he ever attack you?'

'No, but he was one of those who said I had abused Stephanie after she left me and before you ask, I never attacked him either, although I was tempted to on more than one occasion.'

Edna Lockheed took up the dialogue.

'James Dickinson was a huge disappointment to his father, Judge Dickinson. James never amounted to anything and as far as I'm aware has never worked for a living, but he did have one of his father's traits in that he interfered with everyone's lives and everything that went on in the village. He married sometime after Stephanie left and they had Peter, but the marriage didn't last long. His wife struggled with his controlling behaviour and she left him, taking Peter with her. Dickinson's attitude then got considerably worse. You would turn around and he'd be there. He came to all the village events and took over. He was, to put it bluntly, chief inspector, a nutter. A good reason for not letting him near Jennifer.'

Cornell looked at the girl. She was oblivious to the conversation and Max wondered if she was partially deaf. Joseph Lockheed picked up on his curiosity.

'Jennifer came out of the crash completely unscathed, at least physically, which couldn't be said for her parents and brother. But it was three hours before she was cut free from the car wreck and the episode has left her traumatised. She has not spoken since.'

TWO FEET UNDER

Cornell felt sorry for the child. He would have liked to have helped her with the colouring. The purple elephant had been cast aside in preference for a green ostrich, the marks left by the crayon straying far beyond the outline of the bird.

'So, let me get this into perspective,' offered Cornell to Lockheed. 'Dickinson wanted Stephanie, but she married you instead. He was jealous and accused you of her abuse when she left you. His son married one of your and Stephanie's daughters, but they died leaving Jennifer, and Dickinson was suing for custody of her. What am I missing?'

Eleanor Lockheed spoke for the first time and took up the story.

'Stephanie came back two years ago. She stayed at the pub.'

Just when Cornell thought that Stephanie's tale was at an end, something else was introduced.

'Did you see her?' Cornell asked Eleanor.

'No, but my parents did. They have always lived in the village. Although she would be twenty five years older, they said she still looked the same. Same hair do, same style of clothing.'

'Any idea why she returned after twenty five years?'

'It was said at the time that she came to see her daughters,' answered Eleanor.

'And did she see her daughters?' Marty Fielding intervened, which pleased Cornell as he was running out of questions, and possibly the will to live.

'Yes, but the meeting did not go very well. There was no reconciliation,' answered Eleanor Lockheed.

'Did you see her, Mr Lockheed?' asked Fielding.

'Absolutely not. I didn't know she had returned until later when Wendy told me.'

'Did she stay long?' posed Cornell.

'I don't think so, maybe a couple of days,' ventured Eleanor.

'Do you know where she went?'

'No. One minute she was here, the next she had vanished, again,' said Edna.

'I'm not sure what the link between your ex-wife's disappearance twenty odd years ago and her return and second disappearance two years ago has to do with the death of James Dickinson. But I did ask you to explain the history between yourself and the village and you have. If we need to speak to your daughter, Lesley, Mr Lockheed, would you give me her married name and address?'

'No problem. She and Harry, that's her husband, Harry Jamieson, live in Bedson. It's a small village, hamlet really, about five miles away. Turn left out of the farm, first right.'

TWO FEET UNDER

'Well, thanks for the tea and information, all of you. We may need statements from you at a later date, but goodbye for now. Goodbye Jennifer.'

The little girl took no notice and carried on with her colouring in expansive strokes.

James Lockheed showed the two police officers out.

'You never answered whether I was a suspect, chief inspector,' he stated, once he and Cornell were outside and just as there was thunderous bellow from a nearby farm building.

'You are a person of interest, Mr Lockheed. Let's leave it like that for the moment, but what in God's name was that?' probed Cornell.

'One of our Jersey bulls letting you know he's the boss around here. He can smell some of his cows are coming into season.'

'I hope he doesn't think I'm competition!'

Cornell couldn't discuss the case with DC Marty Fielding as the latter went to sleep in the passenger seat within the first two miles of leaving East Hewick for Newcastle.

CHAPTER ELEVEN

Joseph Lockheed watched the two detectives drive out of the farm yard. The younger one acted like a policeman, the older one and the more senior was different to the norm. He was affable and friendly, easy to talk to, asked the right questions, but in such a way that if you had nothing to hide, you wanted to answer them. He was unlike police officers he had dealt with in the past and Joseph had seen many during the foot and mouth outbreak of the early nineties, so many coming on to his farm that he was convinced they would bring the disease with them. Fortunately, by careful planning and ultra-cleanliness, the farm was kept free from contamination.

The destruction of the Jersey herds would have been disastrous. The venture was set up by his grandfather, continued by his father and carried on by himself. They had four herds in various stages of production: milkers, heifers and calves and those ready for sale. The farm also had a five hundred herd of sheep and a small herd of Highland cattle, which apart from the bull, had no economic value. A pastime of his father's, which was the only reason Joseph maintained the herd.

TWO FEET UNDER

Joseph went into the building which housed the bull that had roared such a bellow during the police visit. The animal lifted his head up as Joseph entered and bellowed once more. Did the animal know he was due to be taken out to grass and meet the cows that were coming into season? He was a quiet and friendly animal, with no malice in him whatsoever.

Joseph reflected on the police visit as he led the bull out of his stall to walk the half mile to the field where his ladies awaited. The farmer rarely thought of Stephanie Woods these days. Why would he? She left him with twins to bring up. He never forgave her for that and to this day struggled to comprehend how a mother could leave her new born babies.

But Stephanie was a beauty and he had loved her. He thought she loved him. It was she who led him into the hayshed that day when she came to the farm. Two sixteen year olds, he a virgin. He had presumed she was too, but who knows?

Three months later she announced she was pregnant and everyone, except his parents, told the couple what they must do. This was East Hewick, not the west end of Newcastle. Do the right thing and marry the girl, the vicar said. Correct the mistake in the eyes of the Lord.

That went down well, didn't it?

Stephanie turned out to be lazy, wouldn't get out of bed until the afternoon. Wouldn't help with the egg collecting. No way was she going to help with the cattle. After a row over washing the dishes, Stephanie packed her bags and left for her parent's home.

She stayed with them for a few months, James Dickinson trying his best to attract her attention and starting the rumours that Joseph had beaten her. Joseph went to her parents' home to plead for her return, but she refused to speak to him, nor did she want to see her children. Joseph did not ask her again. In fact he never saw her again. He learned that after a couple of months, she had moved away to live with a relative.

Throwing himself into his work and raising his children, which he could never have done without his mother's help, he gradually learned to live without Stephanie. For a while he forgot about women altogether and for many years never dated anyone. It was at a county show that he met Eleanor Dawson, who was leading the bull in front of him around the show ring. When they stopped for the bulls to be closely inspected by the judges, they spoke to each other.

They spoke later when collecting their first and second prizes and again in the car park as they were leaving. Visits to their respective farms were arranged, which led to further meetings, eventually resulting in the couple becoming engaged. Their marriage was postponed until the twins' marriages. He wished he and Eleanor could have had children, but it didn't happen.

Funny, since Stephanie's return two years ago and although he never saw her at the time, he had not been able to get her out of his head.

And here he was, how did the chief inspector put it? A person of interest in the murder of James Dickinson. Although he wanted the policeman to say he was not a suspect, he got the distinct impression the chief inspector didn't think he was. The village residents however, would think he was the murderer, Joseph was confident of that, but he was equally confident he would not be charged. He had an alibi and witnesses, after all.

CHAPTER TWELVE

Mabel Wainwright was thirty eight years of age. She came from a wealthy family, both of her parents doctors. Her mother now dead and her father, a maturing alcoholic, was well out of the way living in Yorkshire. Mabel did not communicate with him.

Mabel could afford to marry while at university, her husband being ten years older than she and a qualified doctor. Her studies were put on hold for a year after she gave birth to Marian. It was not long after that event, that her husband was offered a position in the USA and sought, without consultation, to move his young family there. Mabel's lack of enthusiasm to work in America caused a rift and the marriage deteriorated rapidly, henceforth ending in divorce some years later.

The husband, duly ensconced as a cardiac surgeon in New York, sent birthday cards and Christmas presents to his daughter, but otherwise took little interest in her upbringing. The two never met again until Marian was sixteen and had developed an obsessive fascination to meet her father. The meeting, only a few months ago, had not been the success Marian had hoped for and she returned home with no aspiration to repeat the experience.

Meanwhile, Mabel had worked in A&E for three years, then fascinated by forensics, took a master's degree after which she spent a further five years in specialist training. Fortunately, a position arose in her home town and she joined Newcastle's pathology and forensics laboratories, rising, through deaths and retirements, to her current senior position.

Doctor Wainwright first saw DCI Max Cornell when he came to the lab to discuss the case of a young man who had been punched by his brother and died. Just one punch but it had connected on the temple causing an internal bleed and death.

The detective had introduced himself with a smile. A smile that shook her. She struggled to give her name correctly and only became composed when discussing the cause of the young man's death.

'It's a bugger, isn't it?' he had said. 'Two siblings arguing about Newcastle United's defence, one clips the other and kills him. He's absolutely distraught. Not a bad lad, just had too much to drink before the match.'

'What will he get?' the doctor had asked.

'For manslaughter? How long will depend on the judge. If he isn't a football fan the lad may get life.'

After the detective had left, Mabel thought about him. Tall, curly black hair, handsome and funny. Most unlike any senior police officer she had ever met. She hoped she would meet him again, and soon.

Her wish was granted with her involvement after the death of a young woman in a seaside town harbour. Max Cornell was the senior investigating officer. Their communications left her wanting to know him better. She returned his friendliness, but remained professional as it seemed he wasn't going to make the first move.

That was down to her, asking him out for a drink followed by an Indian meal. The meeting went well and she learned a lot about him. He joked over his first true love leaving him for an American, but was a little solemn describing the death of his second being shot in the line of duty.

He learned of her parents and her failed marriage, then after a second date, he slept over while her daughter was visiting her father in the States.

From there their relationship grew, and he and her daughter Marian, got on well together. Mabel wasn't sure about his acquisition of a dog, but that aside, she felt herself falling in love with Max Cornell.

TWO FEET UNDER

Six months on and she was becoming desperate, not for his affection, he gave plenty of that, it was an indication of permanence she was looking for, but she wasn't sure she was going to get it. He was known to walk away from certain situations.

She recalled a recent event attended by senior police, the judiciary and the council leaders. He hadn't wanted to go. He hated dressing up, but Mabel's enthusiasm changed his mind. The meal was splendid, the small talk tolerable, two unfunny speeches when everyone laughed, then drinks in the bar of the high end hotel they were attending.

'I say, Cornell, isn't it?' asked a chief inspector from Gateshead, who knew fine well who he was. 'We are just discussing legalising the possession of drugs. What's your stance on it?'

His drinking companions were council officials and a judge. They all looked Mabel up and down, undressing her with every glance.

'The population thinks possession is already legal,' offered Cornell.

'But it isn't,' said the judge. 'It is still a criminal offence. We just don't prosecute possession.'

'So legalising it won't make any difference then, will it? Do you honestly think that the drug problem will go away if it were legal?'

'I say, Cornell, that's a bit much….' voiced the chief inspector from south of the river, but Max

Cornell had already turned his back and walked off to comments of, 'manners, terribly bad form.'

    Mabel Wainwright had made a decision. She had initiated their first date, now she would ask him to move in with her. That was the sensible thing to do. His house, or rather his mother's house in Cullercoats, was too small. Or was it too working class? There was no garage, no utility room, too small a garden. She couldn't possibly live there, he would see that. But what if it was not what he wanted? He had never given any indication of his intentions. How would she proceed? Tell him she loved him?
    She cursed herself. Here she was, dissecting a body to discover the reason for its premature demise and she was acting like a school girl. She would, however, tell him she loved him. Because she did.

TWO FEET UNDER

CHAPTER THIRTEEN

'So, the villagers are not talking?' questioned Mabel Wainwright as she and Max Cornell walked hand in hand along the edge of Newcastle's Town Moor. It was a warm summer evening now, the rain clouds having dispelled and the couple had agreed to a walk to give them an appetite for the meal Mabel had prepared.

Rex, as usual, was off the leash and a hundred metres or so in front of them, sniffing away at messages left by other dogs and occasionally glancing back to make sure his owner was still with him.

'Can't speak for the whole village, Mabel, but those villagers I've interviewed so far are not very forthcoming.'

'How many have you interviewed?'

'Two,' replied Cornell.

Mabel Wainwright looked up at her companion as she so often did, trying to get a sense of whether he was being serious.

'I'm not sure your sample size is sufficient to form a judgement, Max,' she retorted.

'And then on the other hand, Mabel, Farmer Lockheed, who I don't consider a villager, wouldn't shut up and as a result I'm directing enquires about a person who may have nothing to do with the murder of James Dickinson.'

'But then again, might,' she responded.

'That's too subtle for me.'

But Mabel Wainwright didn't want to talk about work. She had one thing on her mind and had thought about it all day. How would he react? Would he walk away? Was she in danger of losing him? She took a deep breath and went for it.

'I love you,' she said.

'I know,' he returned without a moment's hesitation.

There was a silence then. He was still walking beside her holding her hand. He had not walked away, yet.

Please, Max, say something more than that.

She eventually drummed up the courage to ask him where they went from there, but before she could, Rex exploded into a run about a hundred metres in front of them in pursuit of a hare. At first, Rex held his own with the bounding creature, but gradually fell behind the hare's superior speed.

'Rex!' Max shouted. 'Come here you stupid bugger!'

'Please don't let him hurt the poor rabbit,' Mabel pleaded holding on to Max's arm as they watched the chase.

'Mabel, it's a hare not a rabbit and it's perfectly safe,' Max explained, then shouted, 'Rex! Come here! Now!' But the dog ignored him, preferring to run after the hare. Max shouted louder. 'Heel! Biscuits! Walkies! Leash! Marian!'

The dog finally gave up the chase and loped back to his master, tail held high and wagging furiously, obviously pleased at his encounter with the hare. Cornell made a fuss of him when the dog reached them.

'Shouldn't you be scolding him for not coming when you first called?'

'Absolutely not. He would associate being called with punishment.'

'And Marian?'

'He likes Marian.'

Mabel realised the moment of endearment had passed. But Max hadn't walked away and hadn't said anything that would lead her to believe he didn't want their relationship to continue. He hadn't said much actually, other than "*I know*." So her anxiety had been futile if he already knew she loved him. However, she wished she could break down his barriers.

Perhaps on another day.

'How do you tell the difference between a hare and a rabbit?' she asked finally, for want of something to say.

'Hares are twice the size of rabbits and can run ten times faster. I'm hungry.'

'Come on then,' she said. 'I've prepared the meal; just needs to be cooked and it shouldn't take long.'

Max leashed his dog before joining the roadside pavement and handed the leash to Mabel, who reacted with nervousness.

'Come on, Mabel. It's time to take the major step of walking a dog.'

'It would be a damned sight easier if he wasn't so bloody big.'

TWO FEET UNDER

CHAPTER FOURTEEN

Max Cornell had awoken early in the home of Mabel Wainwright to take Rex home to Cullercoats and hand him over to his neighbour for the day.

He would have liked to have taken the dog to East Hewick with him, but it would have been unfair to keep the big German Shepherd in the car all day.

He called in at Alnwick police station on the way to East Hewick to collect a laptop and documentation which Mary Stewart had removed from Dickinson's house. While he was sampling the coffee in the station's small canteen, he asked Mary Stewart if she would check up on Stephanie Lockheed's missing person case of twenty five years ago and if there had been another case opened two years ago.

'East Hewick resident, female, seventeen years old. Maiden name Woods. May be linked in some way to our murder, but don't ask me how.'

'Any relation to the farmer, sir?'

'Ex-wife. Married at sixteen, had twins, then took off.'

He drove to the strange little village wondering if there was a West Hewick. Cornell was to meet Sergeant Donaldson and DC's Fielding, Stainton and Watkins who were travelling in another vehicle to the murder scene.

Arriving at East Hewick before the others, Cornell took the opportunity to look at Dickinson's paperwork Mary Stewart has given him earlier. There were bank statements showing amounts of five hundred pounds being paid in to Dickinson's account now and then and a monthly payment from the Department of Works and Pensions, suggesting Dickinson was unemployed and on benefits.

His two credit card accounts were overdrawn but not seriously so. Mary Stewart had told him she had found a variety of books and much literature on climate change and conspiracy theories such as 911, NASA's space programme, and Princess Diana's death. There was also a letter from Martin, Frame and Bolsover, solicitors in Berwick, confirming an appointment for the following Monday morning.

Cornell's team arrived and Sergeant Donaldson informed him that she had heard Dickinson's post mortem was scheduled for that morning and DC Dennison would attend. Cornell already knew having slept with the pathologist the previous night, but thanked his sergeant for that useful piece of information.

In the graveyard Cornell pointed to the spot where the body had been found and said that forensics thought Dickinson may have been murdered elsewhere and dragged to this spot, but they had nothing other than the piece of a metal watch strap to help them.

'Right,' said Laura Donaldson, 'looks like all we've got at the moment is house to house. So let's get started. All meet in the pub at one o'clock.'

She looked at Cornell for approval and he nodded. Not usual for a DCI to join in house to house, but he had nothing else to do. He was dismayed at the villagers reluctance to talk.

At one o'clock the team met in the *Sword and Lance.*

Bill Walton, pre-warned by Laura Donaldson of their arrival, fussed around them with fresh sandwiches and drinks. The same two elderly men were once again in the corner of the bar engrossed in another dominos session, acknowledging the existence of the officers but totally uninterested in their purpose.

Cornell relayed the story told to him the previous day by the Lockheed's.

'Now, that's thought provoking,' said David Watkins. 'I was invited in to one house by an old lady,' Watkins looked at his notebook, 'a Mrs Agnes Cartwright, to the annoyance of her daughter who lives with her. The old girl has dementia and thought I was her son, Dennis, who, her daughter told me, had been in the army and was killed in Afghanistan about twelve years ago. Her mind was wandering, but she mentioned a Stephanie saying it wasn't right what happened to her. The daughter became uncomfortable after that and asked me to leave, saying her mother needed to rest.'

'I think we should follow up on that,' said Cornell. 'I am getting a bad feeling about this Stephanie. How about you, Laura, anything?'

'I'm getting the vibes, sir, that our presence in the village is making the residents uncomfortable. No one wants to talk to us. I had the door slammed in my face on one occasion, others wanting rid of me from their doorstep in seconds flat. A lot of looking around to see if anyone was watching and a lot of curtain movement.'

'What about Dickinson's house?' Fielding asked.

Cornell informed them of Inspector Stewart's discoveries.

'Two bedroomed semi-detached. According to bank statements, no mortgage, but he did have irregular receipts of five hundred pounds.'

'Where did that come from?' asked Irene Stainton. 'And how come he didn't have a mortgage?'

'Don't know about a mortgage,' answered Cornell, 'but there are no indications on the bank statements where the money came from, so they are obviously cash deposits.'

Cornell glanced at his watch. It was approaching two o'clock.

'I'm not sure any more house to house is going to do any good,' he said. 'What do you think, sergeant?'

'I have to agree, sir. We already know who died. Everyone knew him, everyone hated him. We know he loved a girl who married someone else and who subsequently went missing but returned a couple of years ago, then went missing again. I'm not sure whether there's a link in all that or if it's just clouding the issue.'

'Thank you, sergeant. I think I'm even more confused now. Right. Let's get back to the station. We will be there in an hour. This afternoon I want background checks on Dickinson, see if he has a record anywhere and we need to get into his laptop. I also want a financial check on Joseph Lockheed to see if he is drawing the occasional five hundred pounds in cash.'

CHAPTER FIFTEEN

The murder investigation team members assembled in their incident room later that day and sat in front of the whiteboard, noted with information of what they knew of the case, which was very little. Chief Superintendent Blakeshaw joined them and sat at the rear. Cornell would have preferred him not to be there as his presence, he thought, could stifle comment but at least he was showing interest in the investigation.

'DC Dennison,' began Cornell, 'tell us about the autopsy.'

'Yes, sir.' Dennison was the youngest member of the team. Previously in traffic, where he had a propensity for writing off police vehicles. He often came across as immature, but he also displayed the attributes of a good detective on occasions.

He referred to his notebook. 'Doctor Wainwright performed the autopsy on James Dickinson. There were five stab wounds in the chest and abdomen. Four not considered fatal but a fifth entered the heart sufficient to damage it irrevocably, which is the cause of death. It could, however, have been anything up to an hour before he finally succumbed to his injuries. Doctor Wainwright thought the knife blade was twelve and a half centimetres long, two and a half centimetres wide and very sharp.'

'What about his attacker, anything to go on there?' asked Sergeant Donaldson.

'The attack was from behind, Sarge. Doctor Wainwright thinks the murderer held Dickinson around the neck and stabbed like this.' Dennison exhibited holding someone around the neck and stabbing, using his pencil. 'The knife strokes were inclined to the left which suggests the killer was left handed. The attacker, the doctor thought, would be tall and strong, probably male but the doctor is not excluding female. No foreign DNA on the body. Dr Wainwright will be emailing her report tomorrow, sir.'

Laura Donaldson added the relevant information to the whiteboard and all eyes turned towards Cornell for the next move.

'There is nothing to suggest that the murderer is not an East Hewick resident and if so, somebody in East Hewick knows something about it. Laura, I want you and Irene to go and see Lesley Jamieson tomorrow. Now that we know about her mother Stephanie, I'm interested to know about her visit here two years ago and whether there is any connection to Dickinson, he being infatuated with her. Also, how Lesley feels about her father being a suspect in this murder. Marty and I are going to have a chat with this Mrs Cartwright,' confirmed Cornell.

'Good luck with that, sir,' said Watkins.

'Thank you, David. When is your wife due?'

DC Watkins looked at his watch.

'In about two days, thirteen hours, six minutes and fourteen seconds, sir.'

Everyone laughed at Watkin's precision, knowing although his answer was humorous, the time of birth would have been calculated exactly nine months from conception.

'Shouldn't you be on some kind of paternity leave?' queried Cornell.

'No bloody way, sir. Her mother has come to stay with us and is in total command. She has had the hospital journey planned with military precision since Amanda told her she was pregnant.'

DC David Watkins had just turned thirty. Always immaculately dressed in collar and tie, even in the height of summer when most of his colleagues were in short sleeve order. He suffered from OCD and everything on his desk was ordered in such a fashion that if anyone moved anything so much as a millimetre, and DC Dennison often did so to annoy him, he would know immediately. He was married to a domineering wife who had decided nine months ago that they would start a family.

'OK, David,' said Cornell, 'but you are office based until you decide to leave us. Peter, contact Martin, Frame and Bolsover, the solicitors in Berwick to see what Dickinson's appointment was all about. Also, if you have time, find out what you can about East Hewick. There must be some reason why the residents are so bloody obstructive.'

Cornell then remembered Blakeshaw at the rear.

'Sir, would you like to say anything at this stage?' asked Cornell.

'Thank you, chief inspector, if I may.' The superintendent arose from his seat and walked to the front. 'From what I've heard this morning, this Joseph Lockheed is our main suspect and as such, I think he should be under arrest and in custody.'

'Sir,' Cornell interrupted, 'he is not the murderer.'

'Sounds like he has sufficient motive to me. However, I will leave that with you for the time being. You say that our presence in this village is making the residents uncomfortable and in some instances obstructive. I shouldn't have to mention, but be careful and don't upset anyone. The press will be looking on and I don't want any mishaps. I understand some of you will be staying in the village for a little while, so don't overdo it. We need to remain within budgets so I will be keeping an eye on your expenses claims. That's all.'

The chief superintendent didn't retake his seat, rather left the incident room for his office.

'Thank you, sir,' said Cornell, refraining from commenting further on his superior's input, but it didn't stop DC Fielding muttering away.

'That was encouraging,' the constable said sarcastically.

'As much good as an ashtray on a motorbike,' added DC Dennison.

'DC Dennison, I heard that,' chastised Cornell. 'For your transgression, give Bill Walton a bell and see if he can accommodate four singles in his pub.'

TWO FEET UNDER

CHAPTER SIXTEEN

The July day was already hot with not a cloud in the sky. Cornell had been up early and after taking Rex for his morning walk, had dropped him off at Mabel Wainwright's, to the delight of her daughter.

'It wouldn't have been my suggestion, Max,' said Mabel, 'but Marian's bored with the school holidays and seeing the same friends and doing the same thing day in day out. Looking after Rex will give her some variation in life. Thank you.'

Cornell's passenger north was Marty Fielding, and for a reason. Fielding, while appearing to get on with the rest of the crew tended to avoid conversation with Cornell. He moved into the front passenger seat once Rex had vacated it.

'How are things going, Marty?' asked Cornell as they headed for the A1.

'OK,' was the response.

'Come on, Marty. You will have to do better than that.'

Fielding shuffled in his seat, obviously uncomfortable with the question.

'It's difficult,' he said.

'What's difficult?'

'Let it go, sir.'

'No, I won't. Not while you are in my team. So what's difficult?'

'I lost my stripes, sir,' Fielding announced, 'and that's made things difficult at home.'

'Wouldn't your dismissal have made things a whole lot worse? What did you do anyway? I know the charges against you, but not the basis for them.'

'It wasn't anything, sir.'

'It must have been. Tell me.'

Marty Fielding sighed.

'Do you know WPC Sharma, sir?'

'No. Probably seen her, but don't know her. Sounds Indian.'

'She is, sir. Well, she had just come back from leave. Been home to India with her husband for two weeks. I asked if she'd had a good fortnight and she claims I said she must have had a good fortnight, referring to her colour as a sun tan.'

'Why would she say that?'

'We had words a few weeks before, sir. She didn't take it well. Got her own back, I suppose.'

'You thought of appealing?'

'They didn't believe me first time round, sir. It was just her word against mine. They believed her. Why should they listen to me next time?'

Cornell decided he would look into the case. On the one hand he had Owusu who claimed he was racially abused every day and on the other, was someone who appeared to have had the tables turned on him.

'How are you getting on with Sergeant Donaldson?'

There was a pause in the conversation as Fielding transferred his thoughts to the sudden change of subject.

'I feel she is testing me all the time, sir. It's not easy.'

'So, how are we going to handle Ethel and Agnes Cartwright?'

Fielding paused once again at another subject change, but attempted to answer.

'The first problem will be gaining access to the house, sir. The daughter will try and keep us out. If we do get in, I think it would be better just to let the old dear talk.'

'I agree. So, you take the old dear and I'll have a word with the daughter.'

'Yes, sir. Thank you, sir.'

'My mother isn't well,' said Ethel Cartwright. 'You can't come in. She is resting.'

'Who is that?' said a very much awake woman's voice from inside the house. 'Who is at the door, Ethel?'

'Your mother talk in her sleep?' asked Cornell mockingly.

Ethel Cartwright shouted back. 'It's nobody, mother. I'll be in in a minute.'

'But I heard a man. Is it Dennis? Has Dennis come back?'

'No, mother. It's not Dennis.'

'Then who is it?' her mother insisted.

'Perhaps you should let us in, Miss Cartwright,' suggested Cornell. 'Make it easier to explain to your mother.'

Ethel Cartwright looked out into the street, right and left. There was no one in sight, but Cornell had no doubt there would be watchers from behind the curtains of the adjoining houses and those opposite. He and Fielding entered the house, the constable continuing on into the lounge.

'You are not Dennis,' said Agnes Cartwright as Marty Fielding sat down opposite her.

'No, ma'am, I'm not.'

'You look a bit like him though. Did you know him?'

'No, but I would like to know about him. Can you……'

Cornell closed the door from the kitchen to the lounge and sat down at the dining table gesturing for Ethel Cartwright to do the same. She was not happy at all and kept looking at the lounge door, but she did sit down.

Cornell began talking to Ethel about the village, the church, the school, what she did for a living and about her life in East Hewick. She answered mainly in words of one syllable, giving nothing away and once again Cornell had to patiently drag the answers out of her. Eventually, after some thirty minutes, Cornell asked the question.

'What's this village hiding, Ethel?'

'I don't know what you mean,' she replied, a little too quickly.

'Yes you do. There's been the murder of a resident who was known to everyone in this village and no one wants to talk about it. It's like some people are frightened we unearth something bad that happened in the past. Am I right?'

'I don't know what you mean,' she repeated. 'I had nothing to do with James Dickinson.'

'When did you last see him?'

'I can't remember. I don't keep a record of who I meet. Now I must get back to my mother.'

'She's all right. She's chatting away to my detective constable. Do her good to talk.'

'Won't do you any good, though. She has dementia. She doesn't know what day it is.'

'Yes, but I understand some people with dementia can remember what happened in the past with clarity. That's what you're worried about, Ethel, isn't it?'

Ethel Cartwright continuously rubbed her hands together, then touched her lips, her chin and cheek all in succession. Something was really troubling her. She suddenly stood up and shouted.

'You have no right to keep me from my mother! It's harassment! I want to see my mother and I want to see her now!'

'Alright, alright. Calm down.'

Cornell could see Ethel Cartwright was in no mood to continue being questioned. He would have to give her access to her mother. He opened the door to the lounge. Marty Fielding was already on his feet.

'I heard,' he said to Cornell.

'And you come around and see me again, young man,' Agnes Cartwright commanded.

'I will, Agnes. It's been very nice talking to you. Goodbye ma'am,' returned Fielding, shaking hands with the old lady.

'Goodbye, Dennis, and be a good boy.'

The two officers left the Cartwright house and walked off in the direction of the *Sword and Lance.*

'God, that was hard work,' said Fielding.

'Get anywhere?'

'Well, I know what weight Dennis was when he was born and which schools he went to, then I asked her if she knew Stephanie Woods and the old lady went a bit solemn.'

'How do you mean?' asked Cornell.

'Well, for a couple of minutes she seemed perfectly rational and asked me if I knew that Stephanie had come back. I said I did know, but I'd heard she had disappeared again. Agnes said something like, "*it shouldn't have happened. It was that devil. Wouldn't let things go.*"

I asked who "that devil" was, but she wandered off again talking about Dennis. What about you, sir?'

'It was pretty obvious,' Cornell answered, 'that Ethel was concerned. No, it was more than that, she was terrified that her mother would reveal something to you. It's my guess, Marty, that something happened in this village. Something bad. Whatever it was, it is somehow linked with James Dickinson's death and I'm beginning to believe Stephanie Woods or Lockheed is involved in it too.'

Ethel Cartwright answered the phone.
'What did you tell them?' the voice asked.
'I didn't tell them anything,' replied Ethel.
'What about your mother?'
'I don't know what she said. She was in another room with another detective.'
'Bloody hell. That was a big mistake.'
'I couldn't help it.'
'You stupid bitch. Your mother will give us all away with her rambling on.'

'Well you should have thought about that before now. My mother didn't cause the problem.'

'But she was part of it, just like the rest of us.'

'And we have to live with it. Now don't call me anymore. I don't like your attitude.'

Ethel slammed the phone down.

Cornell's mobile rang. It was Inspector Mary Stewart from Alnwick.

'Found the misper file on Stephanie Lockheed, or Woods, sir. When she left Joseph Lockheed, she had initially moved back in with her parents in East Hewick, but was being stalked by James Dickinson to the point that she had to move away. She went to live with an aunt in Darlington, where she was living when the police found her. She didn't want anyone to know where she was. She had left East Hewick in 1993 because she couldn't cope with marriage and parenthood. The police officer who interviewed her at the time documented that he was surprised and somewhat troubled that she was not interested in her children, who she'd left with her husband.'

'Thanks, Mary. And what about two years ago? Was there a missing person's case raised then?'

'No, sir, but one of my officers recalls an enquiry about a Stephanie by a firm of solicitors from Darlington, but the surname was neither Woods nor Lockheed. Nothing became of it.'

TWO FEET UNDER

'OK, I'll get Peter Owusu to try and track her movements from when she arrived in Darlington in the early nineties. I can't have too many officers looking at this as it may all be a red herring.'

Cornell rang Peter Owusu and asked him to try and track Stephanie Lockheed after she arrived in Darlington.
'Boss, I've been trying to ring you. I've been in touch with Martin, Frame and Bolsover, those solicitors in Berwick who Dickinson had an appointment with on Monday next.'
'Anything?'
'The solicitor Dickinson was to see was a Donald Peston. I was put through to him, but he told me to mind my own business and rang off. I tried to ring him back, but he was suddenly not available.'
'I think we should follow up on that one, don't you, Peter?'
'Yes, sir. Sounds a bit fishy.'
'Right, leave that with me.' Cornell killed the call. 'Marty, with me.'
'Where to, sir?'
'Berwick.'

'It's for you,' said Ernest Hume holding the receiver out to his wife.
'What?' asked Gladys.

'I've just been on to Ethel. The police have been to see her and her mother. They were interviewed in separate rooms, so God only knows what Agnes told them.'

'Agnes doesn't know what year it is and all she wants to talk about is Dennis. I don't think the police will be interested in that.'

'Aye, if that's all she talked about.'

'So, what do you want me to do about it? Why are you ringing me anyway?'

'Somebody's going to let something slip. I'm going to have a word. We can't go on like this.'

'Well, good luck with that. I can't wait to see the reaction.'

Gladys Hume returned the receiver to her husband who placed it on the cradle.

'Don't tell me. I don't want to know,' he said, standing up from his seat and leaving the room in favour of the office.

Gladys shrugged her shoulders.

CHAPTER SEVENTEEN

'He's had to go out,' said the brusque, middle aged female receptionist at Martin, Frame and Bolsover, who, Cornell noted, was not wearing a wedding ring. Hardly surprising, he thought.

'When is he due back?' asked Fielding.

'I don't know, he didn't say.'

'Has he cancelled any appointments for this afternoon?'

'I can't possibly give you that information.'

The receptionist was of the type Cornell had met before; most protective of those she served.

'Who is the senior partner here?' asked Cornell.

'That would be Julien Frame.'

'Is he in?'

'You can't see him.'

'Why not?'

'You don't have an appointment.'

Cornell bent forward and spoke quietly.

'It's possible I don't need an appointment, ma'am. You see, when investigating a crime, the police don't need appointments and I'm investigating the serious crime of the murder of a Mr James Dickinson, a client of yours, who had an appointment with your Mr Peston on this coming Monday. The purpose of that meeting may assist us with our enquiries in tracking down the murderer. Now, I would be ever so grateful if we could speak to the senior partner.'

Cornell wrongly thought his gentle approach would help.

'I can make an appointment for you with either Mr Frame or Mr Peston, but not both, and Mr Frame has no free appointments until Tuesday.'

Cornell, shaking his head, turned to his constable.

'I don't believe this. Why is everyone in this part of Northumberland so bloody obstructive, DC Fielding?'

'Might have something to do with the county being subjugated by the Vikings in the eighth century, sir. Some people never got over it.'

Cornell let that one go.

'OK, this building has three floors. Marty, you take the top floor and I'll take the first. Ring my mobile if you find our Julien. I'll do the same.'

The two officers turned towards the stairs and a frantic receptionist left her fortress of a reception area, shrieking at the two men who were violating her authority.

'Call the police,' said Fielding over his shoulder as he took the first step.

TWO FEET UNDER

Cornell was pleased to see that office doors on the first floor displayed the names of the occupants. He spotted Donald Peston LLB and opened the door. The office was untidy with files littering the desk and the floor space in front of it. It was also empty. Seconds later his mobile rang. Cornell pressed the green button.

'Up hear, sir,' came the voice on speaker.

Cornell took the stairs to the next floor two at a time and met Fielding, following him into an office where the occupier stood behind his desk with a mobile telephone in his hand. As well as Fielding disturbing him, the receptionist had obviously been in contact.

'I'm fairly sure you and your colleague are committing a criminal offence,' said the senior partner, surprisingly calmly. He was elderly, but with his hair dyed to a severe shade of dark brown. He wore an immaculate navy blue, pin stripe suit with matching waistcoat and fielded a perfectly shaped Windsor knotted, plain coloured tie. He sat down in his huge leather chair and gestured for the two officers to do the same in the more mundane seats in front of his desk.

'I'm fairly sure you are right, sir,' agreed Cornell. 'I am DCI Cornell, this is DC Fielding, and we are investigating a murder. Enquiries led us here and we need to talk to someone. Your associate Donald

Peston was totally uncooperative when we contacted him earlier today and now doesn't appear to be in the building, hence the reason we asked for you. The drag..., sorry, your receptionist obviously believes protecting you from inquiry is more important than solving a murder.'

'That's true, chief inspector. The dragon can be very protective. So, what can I do for you, before I report you to the chief constable?'

Julien Frame considered his visitors. The constable had a stern expression, while his senior was actually smiling.

'The murder victim,' Cornell began, 'namely James Dickinson of East Hewick, who met his demise three days ago, had an appointment with your Donald Peston, Monday next. The purpose of that meeting may help us with our enquiries.'

'You know we cannot divulge that, chief inspector.'

'Mr Frame, James Dickinson is dead, he is unlikely to report you to the Law Society for breach of confidentiality.'

'But his estate could. However, I take your point. I will have a look and see if there is anything I can help you with.'

Frame turned to his laptop and brought it to life. 'While we still work with paper files, chief inspector, we do have a digital appointments system and after many years I have finally mastered it. Now let's see... Monday. What time?'

'The letter Dickinson received requested he attend at ten thirty.'

The senior partner pressed a number of keys on the laptop.

'Yes, chief inspector, Donald Peston does, or should I say did, indeed have an appointment with James Dickinson on Monday at ten thirty. However, I'm surprised Peston hasn't cancelled it if the man is dead. I shall have to speak to him about that.'

'He may not know of James Dickinson's death yet,' offered Fielding.

'That would surprise me,' returned Frame. 'Peston lives in East Hewick.'

'That's interesting,' responded Cornell. 'Does your digital appointments system tell you if Dickinson has been in these offices before?'

'Most definitely and any paperwork would be referenced as well. Just a minute. Yes, here we are. A James Dickinson was seen by Peston on a previous occasion two months ago. There is also a file referenced.'

'May we see that file?'

'I suppose you will get a search warrant if I refuse.'

'Something like that. Look, I don't want to remove the file from the premises. I just want to look at it, or for you to tell me what it's about.'

Frame gave a huge sigh then made a call to the general office for someone to trace the file and bring it to him. It took only five minutes. Frame opened the file.

'It appears Donald Peston was acting for James Dickinson in a custody case for his granddaughter, Jennifer, who is currently living on a farm with her other grandparents called Lockheed.'

'How far has the case got?' asked Cornell.

'It seems Peston has drawn up the paperwork in readiness to apply to the courts. The purpose of the meeting on Monday was to agree the contents and take a copy of Dickinson's passport and a council tax bill to comply with fraud regulations.'

'How long has Mr Peston worked here, Mr Frame?'

'And the relevance of that is?' asked the senior partner.

'I'm not sure at this stage. May not be relevant at all,' said Cornell, 'but it will save us coming back if I need to know.'

'He has been with us for just over a year, maybe eighteen months. If you need the exact date you will have to take it up with the office.'

'Mr Frame, what do you know about East Hewick?' asked Cornell.

'As I understand it, chief inspector, it's a small village between here and Alnwick, but I know no more than that. I cannot recall the last time I travelled through it and I have never had cause to stop there.'

'Can you give us Donald Peston's address in East Hewick? We will find it anyway, but you could save us time.'

The solicitor sighed but acquiesced and Cornell and Fielding left the solicitors office promising not to bulldoze their way in again and Frame giving his assurance of cooperation in the future.

'Where do we go from here, sir?' asked Fielding.

'Let's call in at the local nick. It's just around the corner. The inspector there, Shaun Lambert, used to be at Alnwick. He may be able to throw some light on East Hewick, but it's interesting to know that this Peston lives there.'

'It's good to see you, sir,' said Inspector Shaun Lambert, after answering how he was getting on following his transfer from Alnwick. 'Loved what you said in court during the Symonds trial the other day. We all had a good laugh.'

Cornell introduced Fielding.

'We are investigating a murder, Shaun. A James Dickinson, resident of East Hewick. Heard of him?'

'Can't say that I have, until I heard the news on Tuesday night. Thought his picture looked a bit familiar but I couldn't recall why.'

'What, if anything, can you tell us about East Hewick, Shaun? I realise it's not on Berwick's patch, but you would know of it from Alnwick.'

'Ah, the mysterious village,' Lambert responded. 'Population about five hundred and decreasing. Younger element moving away for work. Low crime rate. I seem to remember a minor burglary when I first moved to Alnwick years ago.'

'Does the name Stephanie Woods, or Lockheed ring any bells?'

'Seem to remember an enquiry from a firm of solicitors about a Stephanie from East Hewick a couple of years ago, but the surname wasn't Woods or Lockheed. I can't remember what it was. Sent a couple of the lads there to look into it but they came back saying it was a waste of time. Nobody knew anything, apparently.'

'You said mysterious village, Shaun. Why do you say that?'

'Looks a nice village from the outside but it's never been a great place to visit, sir. Other villages in the northern part of the county are friendly. They talk to strangers as if they weren't strangers. They will offer help with directions and places to visit. East Hewick is the opposite, they won't give you the time of day and I heard it had got worse these past couple of years.'

'Any reason why, Shaun?'

'Don't know, sir. You hear these things, but don't take much notice of them.'

'Do you know anyone who lives there?' asked Cornell.

'Just the Lockheed's on the farm. Was this Stephanie Lockheed related to them in any way?'

'Married to Joseph for a short time when they were both sixteen. It was back in the early nineties. She couldn't cope and left, but came back to the village about two years ago for a couple of days. That must have been what the enquiry was about.'

'Could be. I remember Joseph from the "Foot and Mouth" outbreak in the late nineties. He was one of the few farmers around here who managed to keep his herds safe, but the villagers kept reporting that the farm was infected. I don't recall him being married at the time.

'Who was reporting him?' asked Cornell.

'Now, let's see. The postmistress was fairly vocal, and another chap who was an interfering busy body.'

'Sounds like Dickinson,' offered Cornell.

'The guy that was just murdered, sir?' queried Lambert.

'Possibly.'

'So what happened?' asked Fielding.

'Nothing. The farm was regularly inspected to no avail, then "Foot and Mouth" died out.'

Sergeant Donaldson rang while Cornell and Fielding were driving back to East Hewick.

'We've been to Bedson, sir, and spoken to Lesley Jamieson.'

'How did it go?' asked Cornell.

'Lovely little village, sir, more of a hamlet really. There is no pub. It was a difficult visit, sir. A dog that wouldn't stop barking and two very young children yelling and fighting. However, Lesley Jamieson doesn't think her father would murder James Dickinson. He's all bluster, she says, but soft on the inside. There was animosity between him and Dickinson that goes back years to when they were at school together, but got worse when her sister Wendy married Peter, James Dickinson's son. Peter and his mother, Dickinson's ex-wife, had moved to Cornhill.'

'What about preventing her father's valuable herd of Jersey cows from being milked. Couldn't that have driven him to violence?'

'Not according to Lesley. He would have lost his temper at the time and hurled threats, but after the event he would have calmed down. She said he never held grudges.'

'Was Lesley aware of her mother's return two years ago?'

'Yes, sir. She thinks her mother arrived in East Hewick on a Friday in September, she can't remember the exact date. She wasn't aware of her being here until the Saturday afternoon when her sister Wendy rang to tell her. At the time, Lesley was working on the farm, which included Saturday mornings. They were to meet their mother in the village hall on the Saturday night.'

'Did they go?' asked Cornell.

'Yes, sir, but Lesley said her mother was drunk and she started slagging off their father and grandmother, which didn't go down at all well with the girls. The meeting didn't last long with the twins soon leaving and Stephanie shouting after them from the doorway of the village hall that they were rubbish, just like their father.'

'Then what?'

'Stephanie must have told the landlord of the *Sword and Lance,* Bill Cash, about her twin daughters because he rang Lesley up the following week demanding she pay for her mother's stay in the pub. Lesley of course refused, as did her sister.'

'Anything else?'

'Only that a solicitor called Peston approached her and her sister last year seeking information about Stephanie. They told him the same story.'

'Why was Donald Peston enquiring about their mother?' asked Cornell.

'She didn't know, sir, and didn't ask.'

TWO FEET UNDER

CHAPTER EIGHTEEN

Cornell parked his car in the pub car park and he and Fielding entered. Walton, like any good landlord had learned what they drank and pulled their beers without asking.

'Bill,' said Cornell addressing the tenant, 'about two years ago, before your time, a lady named Stephanie Woods or Lockheed booked in here. She disappeared into thin air after a couple of nights and might have left behind something. You haven't found anything in the pub that could have belonged to her, have you?'

'No way, chief inspector. I've been right through this pub and the living quarters with a fine tooth comb and a bucket of Domestos. It was bloody filthy when I got here. In fact, until I cleaned it up, I used to wipe my feet on the way out. There was nothing I found that would fit that bill, I'm afraid. However, I do still have the old register. By law you have to keep them for five hundred years or thereabouts.'

Walton disappeared through the back and they heard his rapid footsteps going up the wooden staircase. Two minutes later they heard his return. He placed the register, fairly battered and dusty, on the bar and opened it.

'Have you got a date?' he asked.

'Try September 2017,' said Cornell.

Walton turned a number of pages then when he found September he ran his finger quickly down the list of names. His finger suddenly stopped, then he tapped the register triumphantly.

'Here's a Stephanie Woods.'

He turned the register around so Cornell and Fielding could see the entry for Stephanie.

'It seems she was about to write something other than Woods,' said Fielding, pointing to a mark between her first and second names. What is that, sir?'

'Could be the start of a P, R, or even a B. Doesn't look like an L for Lockheed, does it? I wonder if she remarried but decided not to write her married name in this register.'

'Who is this Stephanie Woods Lockheed anyway?' asked Walton.

'Joseph Lockheed's first wife,' said Cornell. 'Ran off when they'd only been married a few months and left him with their kids.'

'I've heard that story in the bar. A bit of a scandal at the time.'

'Do you know the pub's previous tenant, Bill?' asked Cornell.

'Not really. He was called William Cash. Still lives in the village actually, but he's never been in here since I've been here.'

Walton left them to tend to customers. When he was out of earshot Fielding asked, 'are you thinking something happened to Stephanie Lockheed when she came back two years ago, sir?'

'I surely am, Marty, and I think it could be the reason why nobody around here wants to speak to us. What is the link we are missing?'

'Sir,' said Peter Owusu, telephoning somewhat excitedly. 'Been on to Darlington nick and guess what? Stephanie Lockheed worked for them as a civilian employee. How lucky is that? The sergeant I spoke to remembers her...'

'How does he remember her, Peter?' Cornell interrupted. 'It was twenty something years ago.'

'Apparently she was bloody gorgeous, sir. His words. She worked there for a couple of years then left. Word was that she met a solicitor through work then married him and moved to Newton Aycliffe, which is about eight miles up the road.'

'Do we know the husband's name?'

'Oh, yes. Are you ready for this, sir? Are you sitting comfortably? The sun will shine......'

'Peter, for Christ's sake.'

'Sorry, sir. She married, wait for it, none other than a Donald Peston. A solicitor with a Darlington firm called Rathbone and Howard. He transferred to their Newton Aycliffe branch about twenty years ago and bought a house there too with his new bride.'

'Wow! Wasn't expecting that,' exclaimed Cornell.

Cornell recalled Stephanie's signature in the pub's guest register. She was about to write Stephanie Peston, then for some reason decided to write her maiden name instead. 'Go on, Peter.'

'So, I called the Newton Aycliffe nick as well, sir, and most of the lads and lasses there knew Donald Peston through police work and his wife Stephanie through being arrested.'

'Arrested, Peter? What for?'

'Apparently, she developed a bit of a drink problem and frequented those pubs she was not barred from on a regular basis. She and her husband were still living in the same house, but their marriage was on the rocks, sir. Aycliffe were aware Stephanie had left the area and a short time later, Donald Peston did too. I contacted Rathbone and Howard, the solicitors he worked for, sir, and they told me Peston resigned from them in 2018 and moved to a Berwick firm.'

Peter, that's bloody good work. Get it on the whiteboard.'

Turning to Fielding who had overheard the conversation, 'what did you think of that, Marty?'

'A bit of a surprise to learn Stephanie and Peston were married, sir. It seems he followed her here. But why? To try and get their marriage back on course? He didn't do anything for a number of months, why did he wait? Why leave his home and come here anyway? Why buy a house here?'

'So many unanswered questions, Marty, until we find what happened to this lady, may or may not be relevant.'

CHAPTER NINETEEN

The team met up at the *Sword and Lance* for their evening meals, to the obvious satisfaction of Bill Walton. The bar was fairly full of villagers too, ostensibly celebrating the end of the working week. A strange phenomenon, according to Walton, as the majority of the population were retired.

Their table however, was sufficiently distant from the drinkers for Cornell to relay the results of Peter Owusu's inquiries.

'So, we are making good progress discovering what happened to Stephanie, which isn't an official investigation, but not making any progress on finding the killer of James Dickinson, which is.'

'Unless her disappearance and his murder are linked, sir,' added Sergeant Donaldson.

'I'm looking forward to what Donald Peston has to say,' said DC Stainton.

'Yeah, but why is he so secretive about it?' posed Fielding. 'Why go to the expense of buying a house here? Why move here? All seems a bit bizarre to me.'

It was decided that after their meal, Laura Donaldson and Irene Stainton would visit Donald Peston, while Cornell and Marty Fielding would visit a Mrs Telford, who had requested the "after dark" visit.

Cornell and Fielding were not about to wait until dark to see Mrs Telford because at this latitude north in the British Isles, darkness didn't descend until after ten o'clock and on moonlit nights like tonight, it never got fully dark at all.

As they made their way from the pub to the Telford address, they met Reverend and Mrs Mavis Mason walking towards them, she linking her husband's arm somewhat awkwardly, being taller than him. They stopped to talk.

'Lovely night, chief inspector,' declared the vicar. 'Have you made any progress with this awful business?' he asked, trying to force a smile and not mention the word murder.

'We haven't got the perpetrator yet, Reverend, but I think we are making progress.'

'Let's hope you catch whoever it is soon, chief inspector,' offered the vicar's wife, 'so we can all sleep safer in our beds.'

'Amen to that, Mrs Mason,' said Cornell.

'Good night to you both,' the vicar said relinking arms with his wife to continue their journey home.

The house Cornell and Fielding were looking for was almost at the end of the village, round a slight bend in the road. There was an aged Morris Marina on the drive, the gate sagged on its hinges and the garden could only be described as unkempt. Fielding pressed the doorbell, its tiny light displaying the name Telford below the bell push.

It took a while for the lady of the house to answer the door and only put a very frightened face around the door when she did.

'DCI Cornell and DC.....'

'I've changed my mind; I can't see you. I don't know anything,' Mrs Telford interrupted, then would have closed the door had it not been for Cornell's foot.

'Don't know anything about what, Mrs Telford?' demanded Cornell.

'The murder. I don't know anything about it. Please, let me close the door.'

Cornell removed his foot and the door slammed shut.

'What do you think we should do now, Marty?' Cornell asked as they both stood staring at the door.

'Well, we could arrange for a SWAT team to abseil from a helicopter and storm in through the upstairs windows, sir, or we could just apply for a warrant. Depends on how much we need to speak to the lady, but I suspect she will not cooperate whichever decision you make, sir.'

'Wonder why the change of heart?'

Cornell's mobile rang.

'Sir, Irene Stainton here. I'm afraid Peston is not at home. The house is empty, although looking through the window it looks lived in. Do we break in, sir?'

'No, leave it until tomorrow. We will call on him early in the morning before he gets a chance to go out.'

CHAPTER TWENTY

Cornell went to bed at about midnight after walking the length of the village and partaking of a couple of pints downstairs in the pub. He had almost drifted off to sleep when his mobile rang. He sat up in his bed and leant across the bedside table to pick up his vibrating phone playing the William Tell overture.

He wondered who it was. *Mabel? No, she wouldn't ring at this hour. His mother? Hardly, she never rang much anyway.*

'Hello,' he answered.

'Max Cornell?' the voice questioned. It sounded American even with just his name.

'Yes, who is this?'

'The name is Jim Carter.'

'Do I know you? And do you know it's after midnight?'

'Sorry about that. It's only six o'clock in the evening here in Washington, DC. You and I have never met, Max, but I know all about you.'

The penny dropped. Jim Carter, Amy Carter's husband.

Why is he ringing?

'Has something happened to Amy?' Cornell asked.

'Yes, but it's not what you might think. As of yesterday, she is very much alive, Max, but something has happened.'

'Why should it involve me, whatever it is?'

'Max, I guess I'd better start at the beginning.'

Cornell sighed and slumped his shoulders. He really didn't want a bedtime story, but his tiredness had been displaced by the phone call.

'I suppose you should.'

'It's all about Todd. He wants to go to college on a basketball scholarship.'

'So why doesn't he? Why would I be interested? He's not my son.'

'I know, Max. You see, he's not my son either. Like you, I did the DNA test too. It seems our Amy was rather promiscuous back then.'

'Obviously.'

'The problem is, Max, as far as basketball is concerned, Todd is not that good. He hasn't impressed any college to sponsor him, so if he wants a career in the sport he will need finance and a lot of it. For example, he would need a private coach. I wasn't about to do that, so Amy came looking to you. That was the reason for our visit to the UK in the winter. Todd is the light of her life, Max. She loves him to bits. He can do no wrong and as far as she is concerned he is the best basketball player since they invented the sport. She didn't take your refusal to help him very well and these past few months have been traumatic for me over here.'

'Jim, it's past midnight. I don't really care that Todd is having a problem getting into college. Why are you ringing me?'

'I think Amy is coming after you, Max.'

'Coming after me? What do you mean?'

'She's out to kill you. Amy has always liked a drink, Max, but these last six months her drinking has got really bad. I think she is taking drugs too as her behaviour can be unpredictable. Yesterday, she and Todd walked out on me after a huge argument.'

'That doesn't mean she's coming here, does it?' queried Cornell.

'Oh, she's coming for you alright. She's talked of nothing else since we returned from the UK, and don't forget, Max, she was once an MI5 agent and she will know how to get hold of a weapon once she gets to the UK.'

'Assuming you're right, Jim, what on earth can she possibly gain by killing me?'

'It's not to gain anything, Max. You rejected her. She had it all arranged in her head that you would cough up the finance for her son. She had Todd's future all mapped out, but didn't count on you destroying her vision. Now you've snubbed her again. Your reply to her last email seemed to send her over the edge. She believes you will have to pay the price.'

'Why are you telling me this, Jim? I was never your friend and you took my girl, and at the time, who I thought was my son, away from me.'

'I feel bad about it now, Max. I didn't then. I was young and stupid. Looking back, my life hasn't been great, centred around Todd for just about everything.'

'Well I can't say I'm too sorry about that, but thanks for ringing. I will think about what you've said and keep my eyes open. Goodnight, Jim.'

'Goodnight, Max, and watch your back.'

CHAPTER TWENTY ONE

At five a.m. Max Cornell awoke, turned over, but couldn't get back to sleep. He lay thinking about the phone call from Jim Carter the previous evening. He was finding it difficult to comprehend that Amy would travel all the way across the Atlantic to kill him. Why would she do that? Killing him would not make the finance she needed for Todd's scholarship suddenly available and she wouldn't benefit from Max's will either. Not least because he didn't have one and Amy could never believe she, or her son, would be beneficiaries anyway. She must know that.

It was seven thirty when he arose and took a shower, during which he heard his mobile ring. When he dried off, he saw the missed call was from Laura Donaldson and she had also sent a text.

Urgent, ring back.

'You rang me, Laura.'

'Yes, sir. Irene and I are at Donald Peston's house and he's not in. It looks just the same as last night. We don't think he's been home, sir.'

'OK, Laura, get back to the pub and we'll decide where we go next.'

'Should we not break in, sir?'

'Hardly, Laura. He's not a suspect, just someone we want to talk to. We'll catch him later.'

Cornell closed the call, to be alerted by another.

'Inspector Lambert, Berwick, here, chief inspector.'

'Hi, Shaun. What can I do for you?' returned Cornell.

'Just had Julien Frame of Martin, Frame and Bolsover on the phone, sir. He has been trying to contact Donald Peston on his landline and mobile since yesterday afternoon. No answer. He's left loads of messages. He says Peston always has his mobile turned on. He is concerned and it's not yet nine o' clock, sir.'

'Thanks, Shaun. Call you back later.'

Cornell killed the call and ran down the stairs of the pub to the public bar. Marty Fielding was sitting eating breakfast and reading a newspaper.

'Marty, with me. Now!' Cornell shouted.

Fielding got up from his table and ran after his boss who had gone to his vehicle. As Fielding got in the passenger side, Cornell told him they were off to Peston's house, although it was only four hundred metres to the solicitors home.

'I fear something has happened to Peston,' said Cornell.

They drove past Donaldson and Stainton, disbelief on their faces at Cornell's vehicle travelling at speed out of the pub car park. Fielding waved, pointing for them to go back to Peston's house.

Cornell explained the emergency to them while Fielding inspected the front door for weaknesses.

'Need a ram for this door,' said Fielding. 'What's it like around the back, Irene?'

'There's a glass panel on the back door to a porch. Then there's another door inside which hopefully may be unlocked.'

'Do it,' commanded Cornell.

Within minutes Irene opened the front door from the inside. Her face grim.

'There's a body on the floor in the kitchen, sir. There's quite a bit of blood.'

'Alright. Everyone stay outside. Laura, get forensics on the phone please.'

Cornell entered the house and walked through the hall to the kitchen. A man, presumably Peston lay in a foetal position on the tiled floor, arms across his chest. The front of his shirt was covered in dried blood and there was a pool of it on the floor underneath him. He was clearly dead and death hadn't just occurred.

Bugger. Should have broken in last night, but never thought for one minute he was in danger. Why is he dead?

Leaving the room without touching the body, or furniture, Cornell made his way to the front door and outside. Sergeant Donaldson passed her mobile to him.

'I have Doctor Wainwright on the phone, sir. I've given her some details.'

'Doctor Wainwright,' said Cornell.

'Chief Inspector. I gather you have a body for me.'

'Are you available?'

'Of course. I hope your lot haven't trampled all over the house.'

'Just Irene Stainton and me. We've touched nothing and will close the house off now. Can you bring a full team up? I want the house turned over.'

'On our way.'

Some East Hewick residents had sidled up to the police tape that surrounded Donald Peston's semi-detached, two bedroomed house. One man, nudging the man next to him and obviously looking for confrontation said,

'If you ask me, you need to look no further than Lockheed's farm.'

'Why do you say that, sir?' asked Cornell.

'Because that Lockheed's bound to have done it.'

'How do you know that, sir?'

'Well he did for Dickinson, didn't he? And if you'd done your job properly, he would have been in jail by now and this guy here would still be alive.'

'How do you know he's dead, sir? We haven't announced anything.'

It was pretty obvious from the police presence and the forensic transport that the situation was serious, but a death hadn't been announced and the man, seemingly embarrassed, slunk away.

Doctor Mabel Wainwright emerged from the house still wearing her protective paper suit. She was hot and the relief at removing her hood was obvious. She signalled for Max.

'Same MO as Dickinson. Stabbed in the chest and abdomen a number of times, the killer standing behind as with Dickinson. Probably the same knife. He's been dead for about twenty four hours. There are credit cards in the name of Donald Peston on the table, also a letter addressed to him. Killer left a footprint. Looks like a size eight or nine, heavy shoe, some fragments of soil there too. Tom Mawson is upstairs going through everything. I will do the autopsy tomorrow morning.'

'You going back now, Doctor?' asked Cornell.

'I thought we could have a bite to eat at this pub you are staying at.'

'Splendid idea. How's my dog doing by the way?'

'He's well looked after and is being exercised and trained.'

'Trained?'

'You may find he reacts differently to you when you see him again.'

Cornell rang Martin, Frame and Bolsover and asked for Julien Frame, to advise him of Peston's death. The senior partner was genuinely shocked.

'Do you know of any next of kin?' Cornell asked.

The solicitor didn't know of any, but would check with office records.

Cornell explained about Stephanie and what he and his colleagues knew of her.

'I didn't know about her, chief inspector, and here's me thinking Peston really wanted to join us. I wish he had confided in me. Perhaps we could have helped.'

'We will need his laptop, Mr Frame, and access to his files.'

'I understand, chief inspector, and the firm wants to cooperate. While you can take the laptop away, I cannot allow you to remove files from this building.'

'That's fine, Mr Frame. We can work around that. We would only be interested in any files pertaining to East Hewick. Please don't let anyone touch the laptop in the meantime. I will send DC Fielding to you tomorrow. I know it's Sunday, but it will also mean no one else is around.'

'That's fine with me, chief inspector.'

Cornell closed the call.

'Marty, you heard that?'

TWO FEET UNDER

CHAPTER TWENTY TWO

The murder investigation team and the county's senior pathologist sat at two tables in the bar of the *Sword and Lance* enjoying their evening meal of chicken and chips, with ice cream to follow.

'I would still like to know what Dickinson was doing in the graveyard before he was killed,' said Marty Fielding. 'I wonder if relatives, maybe a parent, is buried there?'

'James Dickinson's father, the judge, is buried in the graveyard but not his mother,' offered Janet Beveridge the part time barmaid and waitress. She had arrived from the kitchen carrying three dinner plates of food and placed them on the table.

'You lived here long, Janet?' asked Cornell.

'Lived here in the village all my life. I was born here and I've worked in the pub since I was eighteen. The Dickinson family arrived here from Berwick around the mid eighties. The father was a retired judge who died suddenly in the nineties. There wasn't many at his funeral; he was very badly liked. The mother, who was a lot younger than her husband, worked in the post office and shop until 2000 then she moved back to Berwick leaving the house here to James and his family.'

'That was nice of her. That explains why he didn't have a mortgage. But tell me Janet,' inquired Cornell, 'why are the villagers not talking to us? What are they hiding?'

Several punters at the bar turned their heads her way, but it didn't seem to bother her.

'Wait till I get the other dinners,' she said, leaving the bar. She returned immediately with three more dinners, served them and wiping her hands on the cloth she used to carry the hot plates, she sat down at Cornell's table.

'I don't know the answer to those questions, chief inspector. All I can tell you is for the last two years the atmosphere in the village has not been great. It wasn't that great before, to be honest.'

'In what way?' prompted Cornell.

'A young woman who had left the village a number of years before suddenly returned.....'

'Stephanie Woods, married name Lockheed?' interrupted Laura Donaldson.

'Yes,' answered a surprised Janet. 'How did you know that?'

'Did you know her?' ordered Cornell, ignoring her question.

'Yes, we went to school together although we were never good friends. She was pretty, I was plain. She got pregnant at sixteen, was made to marry the father, Joseph Lockheed, had twins then left the area.

Then two years ago, she arrives back in East Hewick by bus and checked in here on a Friday, I can't remember the date or even the month. She was seen all over the village on the Saturday but by the Sunday she was gone.'

'So, she got back on the bus and went home,' proffered Fielding.

'No. That's the thing. She was seen during the Saturday evening after the last bus had gone, and there are no buses on a Sunday. In any event, I don't think she stayed here in the pub on the Saturday night.'

'Where was she seen on the Saturday evening?' asked Cornell.

'Here in the pub early on, but it's known she went to the village hall later.'

'What could be on at the village hall late on a Saturday night?' continued Cornell.

'They have dances every Saturday night, games and quizzes during the week and the occasional wedding reception, all overseen by the church council. Although the village hall belongs to the village, most of what goes on there is controlled by the church for the benefit of the church goers.'

'So you think Stephanie went to the Saturday night dance at the village hall?'

'She was putting it around the pub on the Saturday afternoon that she was going to meet her daughters there, but if you ask anyone who would have been at the village hall that night, you are told in no uncertain terms to mind your own business.'

Janet Beveridge spoke the last part of her sentence loudly, so those at the bar striving to hear would do so, quite clearly. Those nearest turned away.

'Who would be there, Janet?' asked Cornell.

'The church goers mainly. The Saturday night dance, like most things in the village hall was considered a church activity. It was a regular clique and those not in it were not made welcome.'

'Did you know a Donald Peston?' asked Cornell.

'I knew of him. Came in the pub here once or twice.'

'Was he a church goer?'

'Don't think so.'

'What about James Dickinson?'

'Oh, yes. He was a church goer and attended everything else that went on in the village hall. He used to tell everyone that he was in charge of it.'

'Janet, you got any mustard?' asked Fielding, to the annoyance of Cornell who hoped the waitress would continue with her information.

'English or French?'

'English.'

Janet Beveridge left for the kitchen. When she was out of earshot, Mabel Wainwright spoke up.

'She didn't know that Stephanie and Donald Peston were married, did she?'

'That, she didn't,' agreed Cornell.

The waitress returned with a jar of English mustard and a tea spoon.

'Janet,' Cornell asked, 'is it possible you would know the names of those who would be at the village hall that Saturday night?'

'I would know some.'

'Can you give us a list?'

'As soon as I've cleared the tables.'

'Janet,' asked Sergeant Donaldson, 'why have you spoken to us when others haven't and won't?'

'Some of the clique are frightened. I'm not part of the clique and they don't frighten me.'

She left for the kitchen. Cornell wondered about the waitress's last comment.

Why would those in the clique be frightened?

Bill Walton came into the bar, his face red from cooking.

'Bill,' Cornell called him to the table, 'do you know where William Cash lives?'

'No, but Janet will.'

'Marty, get William Cash's address from Janet and go and see him first thing tomorrow. See if he remembers Stephanie and if he can remember anything about her. Does he recall if she returned to the pub from the village hall on the Saturday night. And after we've finished our meal, I think the rest of us should all have a wander around that graveyard,' announced Cornell.

'What are we looking for, boss?' asked Irene Stainton.

'I think James Dickinson was in the graveyard on the night of his murder for a reason. He wasn't killed where he was found, but I don't think he was murdered elsewhere and dragged to the graveyard afterwards. I think he was murdered elsewhere in the graveyard, then dragged to where he was found. Would you go along with that, Doctor?'

'Yes, I would and I would like to help, but I must leave at around nine thirty to get home to my daughter.'

TWO FEET UNDER

CHAPTER TWENTY THREE

It was a warm evening, the sun still shining in the cloudless sky. The graveyard surrounded the church, covering ground on either side with the bulk of the land at the rear. Midges flew in clouds around the search party.

'Right, let's split up,' said Cornell. 'Doctor Wainwright, you take the left of the church; that's where PC Green found a bunch of flowers thrown against the wall. Irene, the right, and we three,' pointing at Donaldson, Fielding and himself, 'will take the rear.'

As they were passing the entrance to the church, the Reverend Mason emerged from his vicarage demanding to know what they were doing in his graveyard at this time of night.

'Our jobs, Reverend. Does the church have a problem with that?' asked Cornell.

'Well, no. It's just that it's unusual to have visitors to the graveyard in the evening.'

'Dangerous too, it transpires.'

The vicar didn't seem to have an answer for that and turned on his heel and headed off towards the vicarage.

After half an hour of searching and finding nothing other than an old used condom, Fielding asked Cornell, sarcastically, if he wanted it bagged. Cornell's phone rang.

'Yes, Mabel.'

'You should see this, Max. Something's not right here.'

'Where are you?'

'To the left of the church where you sent me. What the ....?'

'Mabel!' shouted Cornell.

'Get the hell away from......!' Mabel's voice sounded down the phone.

'Mabel!' Cornell shouted again, the voice on the other end of the phone now distant, then there was silence.

'I think Doctor Wainwright's in trouble,' he cried out to his officers. 'Come with me!'

Cornell set off at a run to the area where Mabel had been searching, it being hidden by the church tower. Reaching the edge of the church in seconds he saw the prostrate Doctor Wainwright on the ground in between two headstones.

'Oh! God, no! No! No! No! Not again!' he shouted in desperation.

On reaching her he saw that the clothing covering her chest was covered in blood, the slash to her throat pumping more, but her eyes flickered. She was alive. Her mobile phone lay smashed beside her. It had been stamped on.

TWO FEET UNDER

'Mabel! Mabel!' he cried, then he was pushed out of the way by Laura Donaldson. She had a handkerchief in her hand and placed it firmly on the doctor's throat to stem the bleeding, at the same time directing her other officers. 'Marty, check the church. Someone has just done this and they can't be far. Irene, look outside the gate. See if anyone is running away. Take photos if you can. Max, call an ambulance, now!'

It was the first time Laura Donaldson had used his first name.

'Yes, yes of course.' He dialled 999. The call was answered almost immediately.

'Emergency. Which service?'

'Ambulance. East Hewick, Northumberland,' He recalled the sat nav coordinates from his first visit to the farm and gave them.

'What is the nature of the emergency?' asked the operator.

'A stabbing. Look.....'

'I will need to call the police as it's a stabbing.'

'I am the police! I am DCI Cornell, Newcastle CID, but call the police if you must after you get an ambulance sent out.'

'Is the victim male or female?'

'She's female, but I don't see what that has to do with it...'

'Is the victim bleeding?'

'Yes, profusely. Now have you got the ambulance under way yet?'

'It will be with you as soon as possible, sir.'

'As soon as possible!' Cornell exclaimed, having fully recovered from the shock of seeing the wounded Mabel. 'You need to do better than that. The victim is a prominent citizen, therefore the incident will be reported on the national news. It would not be in your interest for the ambulance to be delayed, you hear what I'm saying?'

Cornell was sure the operator would have more questions for him, but he closed the call and went to see the victim.

'How is she, Laura?' he asked, trying to be calm.

'She's still breathing,' replied Laura Donaldson, 'but she's still bleeding badly from her throat.'

Donaldson's hands were covered in blood as were her sleeves and the front of her clothing.

'Hell, Laura, you're in a mess.'

Donaldson ignored him.

'She's trying to say something, sir. She's mouthing something beginning with r, and what could be glass, possibly. I can't make it out.'

Cornell looked at the doctor. Her eyes were closed, but she moved her head slowly from side to side. He wondered if she was in pain. Her mouth moved with small pink bubbles breaking on her lips. She was trying to speak; she so dearly wanted to tell Cornell what she had discovered and who had attacked her.

He looked around. There were several gravestones, old looking, obviously this part of the graveyard had not been used for a considerable time. He looked at the names and dates. Most were covered in moss and unreadable. Those he could read were of deaths in the nineteen twenties and thirties. The names couldn't have meant anything to Mabel. It had to be something else. What the hell was it? A siren could be heard in the distance.

'Thank, God,' said Cornell.

'That's one of ours, sir. Ambulances have different sirens.'

'Shit, I've never given siren sound any thought. How is she now?'

'Still breathing, sir, but she's stopped trying to talk.'

Two police cars stopped outside the graveyard and four police officers, including their female inspector, scaled the wall rather than use the gate.

Cornell quickly brought them up to date with what happened. Inspector Mary Stewart offered assistance.

'I want Sergeant Donaldson to remain in operational charge, Mary, but you could help with the

PR. We are going to have press crawling over us very shortly. A murder in a remote village is one thing, but when the pathologist gets attacked it becomes interest on a national scale.'

Another siren could be heard in the distance. This time it was the ambulance. It parked outside the lich gate and two paramedics ran into the graveyard, one carrying an equipment bag on his back, the other pushing a wheeled stretcher.

The sirens brought several villagers, including the vicar and his wife and Gladys Hume the shopkeeper, to congregate on the tarmac path from the gate to the church door. Others, Ethel Cartwright, Cornell recognised, and possibly Mrs Telford. He hadn't seen enough of her face to be sure. Most stood with their arms folded staring at the throng of police and paramedics.

Sergeant Donaldson explained as briefly and precisely as she could the nature of Doctor Wainwright's injuries to the paramedics. One inserted a drip tube into Mabel's arm and as she appeared to be struggling to breathe, the other cut a hole in her throat and inserted a tube.

Not looking good.

After what seemed an age but was probably only a few minutes, Doctor Mabel Wainwright was loaded into the ambulance. Cornell asked if he could go too, and where were they taking her. The paramedic agreed he could accompany Mabel and advised him they were taking her to the Royal Victoria Infirmary, Newcastle, who were experienced with stab wounds.

Laura Donaldson also asked where they were taking Mabel and in full hearing of those villagers who had gathered, Cornell told her Wansbeck General Hospital.

He would explain later, although he suspected Donaldson would work out that the person who attacked Mabel would soon know she wasn't dead and may try and make another attempt on her life.

CHAPTER TWENTY FOUR

Sergeant Laura Donaldson watched the ambulance pull away from the church gate. DC Irene Stainton stood beside her.

'You need to get cleaned up, sarge.'

Donaldson looked down on her bloodied blouse and hands and nodded in agreement.

'I'll go across to the pub now and have a shower. Keep looking around where Doctor Wainwright was attacked. There may be some clue we've missed so far.'

'Bloody hell!' stated the shocked Bill Walton when Donaldson entered the pub, she wishing there had been another entrance to her room upstairs. 'Are you alright?' the landlord asked. 'Is that why the ambulance was over by the church?'

Several nearby punters were listening intently.

'Not for me,' Donaldson retorted. 'Doctor Wainwright has been attacked and taken to hospital.'

She left a silent bar with that comment.

Laura Donaldson watched the pink water gurgle clockwise down the shower drain before she stepped out and draped herself in a large white bath towel. She took off her shower cap and allowed her long blonde hair to shake loose on to her shoulders. Her overnight bag held a spare pair of jeans and a shirt which she placed on the bed.

Once dry she allowed the towel to fall to the floor and she caught sight of herself in the long mirror next to the ensuite door. She was not happy with what she saw. Her body was too thin and her breasts too small. Her mother told her she was pretty, but Laura thought she was just plain. She wished she was as beautiful as Doctor Wainwright, then maybe Max Cornell would notice her.

At university Laura had lived with three other girls, had a relationship with one but that finished when she graduated. She thought she might be gay, but when the opportunity of another such relationship arose, she turned away from it.

On joining the police service Laura Donaldson avoided relationships of any description, throwing herself into work instead. Then DCI Cornell arrived at the station and she was immediately attracted to him. She hoped she would be assigned to his team and to her great satisfaction, she had been.

Max Cornell was unlike any ranking police officer she had ever met, although to be fair, she hadn't met all that many in her relatively short career. He made all his staff feel important, even Ian Dennison, who, given the occasional authority seemed to lose some of his immaturity under Cornell's command. The DCI had been behind Laura becoming a sergeant at what most coppers would deem a very young age. Some said it was only because she was a woman.

'*She's a sergeant because she's bloody good*,' she had heard Cornell say in her defence.

She liked the fact he always asked for her opinion. At first she had waffled and said things she thought he wanted to hear.

'No, Laura. Be honest. Always say what you think. It may get you into trouble now and again, but not with me. I already know what you think I want to hear. Give me something fresh.'

She felt she could speak to him as an equal after that, but remembered with horror that just an hour ago, she had barged him away from Doctor Wainwright in the graveyard. She had even called him Max. That had slipped out. Had he heard it?

Once dressed in her casual attire she went down to the bar. Her colleagues were there, showing surprise that she had discarded her normal formal dress.

'Hey, sarge,' offered Marty Fielding. 'You look good.'

'You wouldn't say that if I was a man,' she returned with a smile.

'Too right. We going to talk about work?'

'I suppose we'd better. Who do you think attacked Doctor Wainwright?'

For the next hour all those villagers known to the team were considered. Especially those who mingled around the graveyard when the ambulance arrived, but at the end of an hour they had both a lot of suspects and none at all.

'Is James Lockheed still in the frame for Dickinson's murder, sarge?' asked DC Stainton.

'Not sure he ever was as far as the boss is concerned,' answered Sergeant Donaldson.

'Still a lot of unanswered questions,' said Fielding.

'We will get on to it tomorrow,' said Donaldson. 'Who's for a game of pool?.'

CHAPTER TWENTY FIVE

The ambulance took off with sirens blaring and Cornell didn't have to suggest they go quicker.

'Hang on,' the paramedic attending Mabel told him. Just as well she was strapped in, thought Cornell as he held on to a handle on the side wall of the ambulance, there for that very purpose.

Then it hit him. Marian. Bloody hell, what was he going to do about Marian?

He thought quickly. His mother.

'OK, to make a phone call?' he asked the paramedic. 'It's not going to stop the instruments working?'

'It's fine,' he was assured. He scrolled down his contacts to his mother's number and tapped it. She answered almost immediately.

'Hello, Max. This is a surprise.'

'Hello, Mother.'

'What's wrong, Max?'

'How do you know anything's wrong?'

'You called me mother. You usually say, "Hi, Ma," as if you had been talking to me yesterday. How long has it been?'

'Please, Ma, I've got a problem. A friend of mine has been badly hurt and I'm with her now in an ambulance going to hospital. She has a daughter at home unaware of her mother's condition. I need you to look after the daughter for a while. She's sixteen going on thirty five and called Marian.'

'Can I speak now?' his mother asked. 'This friend is more than just a friend, isn't she? Else you wouldn't be going to hospital with her and I can tell by your voice you are really worried. That's good, and because she's more than just a friend, I will look after her daughter. When's it to be?'

'Tonight. Will you collect us from the RVI?'

'Yes, what time?'

Cornell looked at his watch. It was precisely eight p.m.

'Be there at about eight forty fiveish.'

'See you later.'

Cornell's next call was to Marian, hoping she was at home. She was.

'Marian, it's Max.'

'Hello, Max, I'm afraid Mother is out on a call at the moment.'

'I know. Marian, listen. I want you to pack a bag of your clothes for a few days and bring yourself and Rex to the RVI in Newcastle.'

'What's wrong, Max? Has something happened to my mother?' she asked anxiously.

'Yes.' Max decided there was use no beating around the bush. 'She has been hurt. I don't know how badly, but she is alive and I'm with her now on the way to hospital. Meet us there as soon as you can.'

He ended the call before she could ask any more questions that he didn't want to answer.

On arrival at the RVI, porters, nurses and a doctor were waiting with a trolley. Mabel was quickly loaded on and whisked away. Max tried to follow, but his way was blocked by a large male nurse who told him in no uncertain terms to wait in the area provided.

Max went outside instead. There was nothing he could do inside. He looked at his watch. It was eight forty five in the evening. His mother should arrive at any time.

'Max!' A voice hailed him from a hundred metres away. He looked up and spotted Marian running towards him with Rex bounding beside her. She must have run the three miles from Gosforth. The big German Shepherd saw Max and rose on his hind legs straining at the leash. Marian, unable to hold him, let him go.

While quieting the excited dog down, Max explained to Marian that her mother had been attacked, but there was nothing either of them could do at the moment as she would be in the operating theatre.

Once her tears has subsided, Marian asked if she could have Rex to stay with her until her mother came home.

'No, I've got a better idea. I've arranged for you to stay at my mother's.'

Marian thought about this. The pet lip protruded.

'So, you think I'm too young to stay on my own, as well.'

'I would have thought you would have considered meeting someone new and inhabiting their living space for a few days as a challenge, allowing you the opportunity to introduce and project your own personality,' said Max, hoping to keep the teenager's spirits as high as possible in appalling circumstances.

'Max, that's crap,' the sixteen year old retorted with a little anger.

'Are sixteen year olds allowed to say crap?'

'So, if I go to your mother's, can I take Rex with me?'

'Of course you can, but there may be a wee bit of a problem. My mother has a miniature dachshund who Rex has never met. He may eat it.'

The teenager was now composed, which pleased Max. Wouldn't have done for her to be hysterical, but he had always found her to be a sensible girl.

'How are we going to get to your mother's?' she asked. 'We don't have a car.'

'She will collect us.'

'When will I be able to see my mother?'

'We'll check now. Tie Rex to that litter bin.'

At the reception desk a nurse with a number of patient files in one arm, used her free hand to make a phone call for them. After a minute she replaced the receiver.

'Doctor Wainwright is in theatre now and likely to be for some time. It is a very intricate operation and too early for a prognosis. There's nothing you can do at the moment. I would suggest you go home and come back in the morning.'

The words "intricate operation" concerned Max, but he agreed with the nurse, it was no use waiting around.

Outside, Elizabeth Cornell stood beside her vehicle with a black and tan miniature dachshund in her arms.

'Hurry up,' she said. 'I don't want a traffic warden spotting my car. Hello Marian, pleased to meet you.'

'Just a minute,' said Max, signalling Marian to untie Rex from the bin.

'What is that?' demanded Max's mother.

'That's my dog.'

'Dog? Are you sure? It's huge.'

'It's a he.'

'So he's huge.'

The little dachshund was barking at the German Shepherd, who ignored the noise and walked to the front passenger seat door, assuming correctly he was going for a ride.

'Err, Rex likes to ride in the front, Ma.'

'In other circumstances, Max, I wouldn't be doing this.'

Elizabeth Cornell opened the front passenger door and the big dog jumped in. Max leaned in and fastened his safety belt. 'I don't believe this,' his mother said, relinquishing charge of Annie the dachshund, her barking having subsided, to Marian who was already in the rear seat. Max got in beside her.

'How is Doctor Wainwright?' asked Elizabeth Cornell once they were underway. Max didn't want to give details of the stabbings. Marian was holding up well, but that knowledge may have a different effect.

'We won't know until the morning. She is having surgery as we speak.'

'What happened to her, Max?' asked Marian.

'Best we wait until tomorrow.'

'I want to know now,' her voice getting louder.

'Tell her, Max,' said his mother from the driving seat. 'She needs to know.'

'She was stabbed, Marian.'
'Where?' commanded Marian.
Max looked at her. Her eyes were full with tears.
'In the neck and chest,' he added.
Marian didn't cry as he expected.
'How bad is it?' she asked.
'It's bad enough, but I don't know how bad, Marian. That will have to wait until morning.'

Elizabeth Cornell pulled her Volvo on to her drive, which drew an exclamation from Marian.
'Wow, what a big house!'
Then behind her hand, Marian whispered to Max asking if his mother was rich.
'Very,' he whispered back.
Over dinner, Max told Marian and his mother of the murders in East Hewick and the attack on Mabel. Marian asked if it was the same person who had carried out both murders.
'It's more than possible, Marian. The murder weapon is a knife and it's likely the same knife that was used to stab your mother.'
'Did my mother put up a fight?'
'You bet she did. If she hadn't, the worst may have happened.'
'I knew she would,' Marian said with pride.

TWO FEET UNDER

After dinner, Cornell made a number of phone calls, one of which was to Wansbeck General Hospital.

Later, almost midnight, Max sat with his mother on a cushioned wooden seat in her garden enjoying a glass of whisky and the mild late evening. To the west the sky was a pale grey colour streaked with orange, against which one had glimpses of swooping bats.

'Annie and I often sit here at this time of night,' said Elizabeth Cornell. 'It's so quiet.'

'Yes, it is kind of peaceful. I can smell a powerful scent.'

'It will be the sweet peas,' confirmed his mother.

Marian had gone to bed and the two dogs were lying at either side of their owners, not quite sure whether they were friends yet.

'Why would anyone attack Mabel?' Max's mother asked suddenly.

'I don't think she was attacked because of who she is, Ma, I think when she called me in the graveyard, she had discovered something. Unfortunately, she didn't tell me what it was over the phone, she just said I needed to see it. The attacker must have been watching her and realised she had discovered something that she wasn't supposed to and decided to deal with her there and then.'

'Do you have any idea who this person is, son?'

'No, I don't. I think this case all hinges on something that happened to a woman who left the village twenty five years ago and came back two years ago, but disappeared after a couple of days. She was last seen at the Saturday night dance at the village hall.'

'Could she have been murdered there?' pressed Elizabeth Cornell.

'That's a possibility. We have a list of some of those who might have been present, but they are not talking and when people don't talk, there has to be a serious reason. There is nothing more serious than murder.'

'Was there an investigation into her disappearance at the time?'

'No. She had no real ties in East Hewick anymore for anyone to report her missing. A firm of solicitors made enquiries later, I think it was her husband acting for himself, but using the firm's name. The enquiry went nowhere and if she had been murdered, her body was never found.'

'So, if she was murdered that Saturday night, what did those responsible for it do with the body?'

Max thought about that. Yes, what did they do with the body? Of course! Sometimes you just need to talk to somebody.

'Mother, you're a genius.'

Max picked up his mobile and speed dialled Laura Donaldson's mobile number. He hoped she wasn't with anyone.

'Max, you can't ring somebody at this time of night,' warned his mother.

'Have to.' The call was answered with a hello. 'Laura, sorry to bother you. It's Max.'

'It's alright, sir. I couldn't sleep anyway thinking about those graves. How is Doctor Wainwright?'

'She was being operated on when we left the hospital. Won't know until tomorrow. Why couldn't you sleep, Laura?'

'One of the gravestones had a marble plinth with a hole in it for a flower jar and a glass flower jar was placed in it.'

Cornell could remember seeing it but had thought nothing of it. There were graves all over the graveyard with flower jars.

'What is so strange about that, Laura?'

'Would you put flowers on the grave of someone who died eighty years ago, even if they were a close relative?'

'Well, I might if they were special,' replied Cornell.

'Hardly, sir. You would not have known them. I scraped away some of the dirt from the gravestone and a Martin Brown, died 1931, is buried in that grave.'

'Maybe Doctor Wainwright will be able to tell us what she found in the morning. I keep wondering about "R.....Glass." Did she see something glass related, or was she attacked by somebody called Glass? Ask Bill Walton tomorrow if there is anyone in the village called Glass.'

'Will do. Sir, is it possible Stephanie Lockheed is buried in one of those graves? The grave of Martin Brown, perhaps?'

'I'm thinking the same, Laura. That's why I rang you. Somebody doesn't want us looking around that particular area of the graveyard. If Stephanie was murdered, burying her in an existing grave isn't a bad way of disposing of the body. Speak to you tomorrow. Get some sleep.'

'Oh, I don't think I'll sleep now, sir.'

Cornell didn't think he would sleep either. Not least because he was no nearer solving the murders of James Dickinson and Donald Peston, but he was certain their deaths and the disappearance of Peston's wife, Stephanie, were connected. He hoped they were.

TWO FEET UNDER

There was also the prospect of Amy Carter turning up at any time and he wasn't sure how he was going to deal with that.

CHAPTER TWENTY SIX

Max, his mother and Marian were being led along the hospital's corridors to the room where Doctor Mabel Wainwright was recovering from the operation to her throat. A doctor dressed in blue scrubs met them at the door.

'How's my mother? How is she?' asked Marian anxiously.

The doctor raised his hands for attention.

'Doctor Wainwright has had a major operation to her throat and repair surgery to her chest. She had lost a lot of blood before arrival, but the treatment was successful in as much as her life is no longer in danger.'

'Thank goodness,' said Marian with a huge exhalation.

'The wounds to her chest are superficial,' continued the doctor, 'however, her throat, her thyroid glands and larynx were damaged. We are concerned about her voice.'

'Oh no! Are you saying she may not be able to speak again?' demanded Marian.

'It is too early to say, but it is a possibility.'

Max put his arm around Marian's shoulders and gave her a squeeze. He couldn't think of anything appropriate to say to her at that moment.

'Can we see her?' Marian sobbed.

'Yes,' the doctor said, 'in a little while. She is being treated by the nurses at the moment.'

They were despatched to a waiting area. Elizabeth Cornell sat with her arm around Marian.

Cornell went to one side and rang Laura Donaldson.

After explaining Mabel Wainwright's medical situation to his sergeant, she brought her chief inspector up to date.

'The press are all over the place here, sir, knocking on doors, following us around. Inspector Stewart is doing a great job, but she can only be in one place at a time. It's not making our investigation easy.'

'I'll get there as soon as I can, Laura. I have a missed call from the chief super. I expect he wants to see me. Must be urgent if he's in on a Sunday. Anyway, William Cash?'

'Marty went to see him this morning, sir. Cash can remember a Stephanie Woods who was booked in for seven nights, but stayed only one. She had told him she was meeting her daughters on the Saturday night at the village hall, but never returned to the pub and he never saw her again. After a week he contacted the daughters, as he had Stephanie's overnight bag and clothes and he wanted payment for the one night. They didn't want to know.'

'What did he do with her clothes?'

'Took them to the village hall jumble sale a few weeks later.'

'I wonder if the people who bought them realised whose they were? Anything else?'

'Marty asked Cash why he never went to the pub now. Apparently it's because the brewery kicked him out as he was purchasing stock from sources other than the brewery and that's not allowed. I think that's a dead trail sir. Oh, I've been on to Peter Owusu who tells me David's wife had a baby girl last night weighing 6 pounds 5 ounces, that's 2.95 kilograms. No doubt we will get the exact specifications later. Also, Janet Beveridge has given us the list of names you requested.'

'Send David and his missus a card from us all, would you? The village shop sells cards. I saw them when I was in there.'

'Already done, sir.'

'Don't know why I asked. Going to see Mabel now. I'll let you know how she is later. Did you find anything in the graveyard?'

'No, sir. Not a thing.'

'Keep looking. We need to know what Mabel saw and I doubt she can give us that information at the moment and probably not for a while. Something possibly glass related. Just a thought; you and Irene try and connect those on Janet's list with the bystanders in the graveyard last night, although I'm not sure how you are going to do that when you don't know all their names.'

'Just as well DC Stainton took a photo of them all then, isn't it, sir?'

'Good for Irene. Speak to you later.'

A nurse arrived and summoned them to follow her, just as Cornell's phone rang. It was Wansbeck General Hospital. He motioned to his mother that he had to take the call.

'DCI Cornell.'

'Hello, it's Sister Dodds from Wansbeck Hospital. Just to let you know that a lady rang the hospital this morning wanting to know the condition of Doctor Mabel Wainwright.'

'What did you tell her?'

'We had to tell her that no one of that name was in the hospital. You have to understand, inspector, that…….'

'It's alright, sister. I don't expect you to lie on behalf of the police, but your vigilance has helped us with our enquiries. Thank you.'

A lady?

He entered the room where Mabel Wainwright lay half sitting up in bed and attached to several tubes of varying diameters delivering fluids to her body and instruments measuring her bodily functions. A bandage covered her throat and bruising from the attack and operation had spread to her lower face. The tube the paramedic had inserted in her throat had been removed and replaced with a larger one inserted through her mouth. Her eyes were semi open but were unseeing.

It was obvious she was not in a position to describe her attacker, or explain what she had found in the graveyard. Marian sat to one side holding her hand. Elizabeth Cornell sat away from the bed allowing her son room to sit near to the patient.

Cornell paused before he sat, looking down at his woman. He knew he should tell her he loved her too, but was too embarrassed in company. He wanted to hold her tightly but had to make do with holding her other hand.

Marian was talking and went on to tell her mother about how big Elizabeth Cornell's house was. She told her mother about the dogs, how huge Rex looked against the tiny Annie, the miniature dachshund.

Mabel's eyes gradually closed altogether. The nurse returned and said it was the effect of the anaesthetic. She asked them to leave, suggesting they come back during visiting hours that evening.

'I agree, but I'm going to organise a guard on her room. No one goes in unless they are hospital staff. Some reporters might try, but Mabel's life may also be in danger.'

The nurse said she would put a chair outside the room for the guard.

Elizabeth Cornell left first, Marian kissed her mother on the forehead, as did Max.

'I've got to go to headquarters, Ma, then back up north. I'm afraid I won't make visiting time tonight.'

'Don't worry, Max. I will look after things.'

Marian walked on ahead to Elizabeth's car. The little dachshund had been left at home while Rex, sitting in the front passenger seat, eagerly awaited their return. 'I don't think you need worry about Rex being looked after either.'

'Thanks for what you are doing, Ma. I really appreciate it.'

'Oh, no problem, son. I've quite taken to Marian. She's a really nice girl. A credit to her mother. But you know that already, don't you?'

The police car Cornell had requested to collect him arrived. He waved goodbye to Marian and his mother and set off for headquarters.

Chief Superintendent Blakeshaw had come into work on a Sunday for the first time since his promotion. When the reporters on his doorstep saw him leave for work in uniform, they would contact the police station rather than continuously contact him at home. In addition, as the senior pathologist had been attacked he thought he should be on duty, although he doubted if his chief inspector would welcome that.

The chief superintendent wrote down everything Max told him about the case on a large A3 paper pad. He had circles and squares around names and lines and arrows drawn between them. Max had seen nothing like it before and hoped it would not become mandatory.

'Doctor Saanvi Patel will be acting chief pathologist for the time being,' said Blakeshaw. 'Do you know him?'

'Yeah, I've worked with him before, sir. He'll be doing the autopsy on Donald Peston, I presume?'

'And any more corpses you discover in this little village, chief inspector. Speaking of which, you believe that this woman, Stephanie Woods, or Lockheed, is buried in one of those graves, don't you?'

'She was called Peston when she died, sir. Yes, I think she is buried in a grave and I think I know which one. It had a flower jar and we found some flowers nearby.'

'You are going to need more than that, chief inspector, if you want the grave opened,' said the superintendent. 'Doctor Wainwright was trying to say "glass" to you in the ambulance. What on earth could that mean? Glass jar? A piece of glass?'

'She was trying to say two words, sir. The first word we think could begin with an r.'

'That's not a lot of help, is it? And you've ordered a guard outside Doctor Wainwright's room. What is she in danger from?'

Cornell explained how he had said in hearing distance of the villagers that they were taking her to a different hospital to the RVI. That hospital had subsequently received a phone call from a woman asking after her.

'It could only have been one of those within earshot when I mentioned it, sir.'

'OK. So, I assume if and when you work out which grave this poor woman is in, you will be seeking a court order to open it?'

'Yes, sir. It should be easy to obtain as we are not exhuming a body, just opening a grave. I doubt if Stephanie is buried very deep.'

'If a body exists at all. At the moment it is only a gut feeling, is it not?'

'Yes, sir. Mine and Sergeant Donaldson's.'

'And you think this will lead us to discovering the murderers of James Dickinson and Donald Peston also?'

'I think they are one and the same, sir, so yes, I think there is a link.'

'Well let's hope so. But here's another problem for you.'

The senior officer handed a newspaper to Cornell open at the middle page and displaying photographs of himself and Mabel Wainwright. The title read, "Should We Be Worried About This Liaison?" Cornell didn't bother reading the article, just the reporter's identity and he wasn't surprised to see the name Jed Temperly. He folded the paper and returned it to the chief superintendent's desk.

'Not going to read it, chief inspector?' his boss asked.

'Just some shit stirring reporter, sir. His comments don't concern me.'

'Well, they concern me and the chief constable.'

Cornell stood.

'I need to be in East Hewick, sir. If there's nothing else?'

There was, but Blakeshaw acknowledged the meeting was ended.

'Keep me in the loop,' was all he could think of to say.

TWO FEET UNDER

CHAPTER TWENTY SEVEN

DC Dennison didn't mind being the only detective in the incident room as it meant he would be in sole charge of serious crime in Northumberland, if only for a little while.

David Watkins was on paternity leave as you would expect, although Cornell wouldn't be surprised if he suddenly walked through the door. He had met David's wife Amanda before.

Later that morning, as his car was still in East Hewick, DCI Cornell was being driven there by DC Peter Owusu, who was pleased to be out in the field. On the way to the strange little village, Cornell filled in the blanks to Owusu's knowledge of the case up to the attack on Doctor Wainwright.

'It seems Peston came north to look for his missing wife and traced her to East Hewick. Marty should have his laptop from the solicitors; I would like you to have a look at it after I show you the crime scene, and where Doctor Wainwright was attacked.'

On reaching the village, Owusu parked outside the graveyard and the two officers walked through the lich gate into the graveyard.

Cornell showed his constable where Dickinson's body had been found and then took him to where Mabel Wainwright had been stabbed.

DC Marty Fielding was there, beckoning the two officers to look where he was pointing.

'I think there are traces of blood here, sir. There may have been more sign of it before the grass was cut.'

'You could be right, but this isn't where Doctor Wainwright was stabbed. That was over there,'

Cornell pointed in that direction.

'So, this may not be Doctor Wainwright's blood, sir.'

'True. Take samples of it, but I'm not sure it's what Doctor Wainwright found. What about around here?'

They stood at the place the pathologist had been attacked.

'Couldn't find anything there, sir. Then I thought I should ask the vicar if he knew who visited one of these graves and put flowers on it.'

'And what did he say?'

'Said he didn't know, which I find strange as every time I've been in the graveyard, including today, he's materialised out of nowhere.'

Cornell glanced at the vicarage. The only window facing the graveyard was a landing window between the floors. Although well into the shadows, Cornell was certain someone was watching.

'Sir!' shouted Peter Owusu who was kneeling down at the grave with the flower jar.

'What is it, Peter?'

'Sir, I think I've found what Doctor Wainwright was trying to tell you.'

Both Cornell and Fielding looked at each other, shrugged, then went to the grave and stood next to the kneeling DC Owusu.

'That was bloody quick. And?' requested Fielding.

'Here, look closely at the grass. In front of the gravestone the grass is different to the rest of the grass. It wouldn't have been too noticeable before as it had just been cut, but now it's grown a bit you can see this grass is of a different variety. It's a much finer texture.'

Both Cornell and Fielding got on their knees to get a better view.

'Bloody hell, he's right,' said Fielding after a few moments inspection.

'Doctor Wainwright wasn't trying to say glass, sir, or a word beginning with r,' offered Peter Owusu, 'she was trying to say grass. Wrong grass.'

'Peter, go to the top of the class,' commended Cornell, taking to his feet again. 'Might be a good idea to pull a few blades of the fine grass and email a photograph of them to Tom Dawson at the lab. Ask him if it's special type and who would use it.'

Cornell took out his mobile and speed dialled his superior.

'Blakeshaw,' said a voice at the other end.

'Sir, it's Max Cornell. We've found the grave, sir, or rather DC Owusu found it, where we believe Stephanie Lockheed might be buried.'

'It's the word "might" that troubles me, chief inspector.'

Cornell explained the difference in grasses and that it looked like the ground had been dug and re-sown with a different kind of grass seed.

'Right, I'll get on to the courts for an order to excavate under your name. I'll stress the need for haste. You will need a digger; I'll get my PA to look for contractors in the area. How are the press behaving up there? Do you need me around?'

That was the last thing Cornell wanted.

'Inspector Stewart is on top of the game, sir. She's keeping the press at a distance. Of course I'm going to have to tell them about the grave excavation, but thanks for the offer.'

Cornell explained to Fielding and Owusu that they were waiting for a court order to open the grave.

'In the meantime, let's go and visit the village hall.'

'Where it all happens on a Saturday night, apparently,' added Fielding. 'But it will be locked at this time of day, won't it?'

'Probably. Who would have a key? The vicar?' suggested Cornell.

'You better ask him, sir. I don't think he likes me very much,' said Fielding.

They knocked on the vicarage door. Mrs Mason answered.

'Do you have a key for the village hall, Mrs Mason?' asked Cornell.

'Why do you want it?' she demanded gruffly, the charm from the previous evening having evaporated.

'To save us breaking the door down,' answered Cornell.

He was getting rather tired with all the procrastination and obstruction they were encountering in the village. Still calm, but he wasn't far from losing his patience. The vicar's wife shouted for her husband and explained the request for a key.

'It will be five pounds an hour,' stated the Reverend Mason.

The three police officers stood stock still and stony faced, staring at the vicar, then Cornell put his hand out for the key. The vicar dropped it in his hand and quickly closed the door.

'What a strange person,' Owusu mentioned.

'Think he's strange? You should see the rest of the villagers,' said Fielding.

The village hall was bigger than it looked from the road and easily capable of handling functions of the type the villagers would participate in.

There were folding tables stacked against one wall and plastic chairs beside them. Cornell's attention was drawn to what looked like a bar in a corner of the hall. On closer inspection, the construction had been well made, its maker obviously a joiner. There were beer, wine and spirit glasses stored on shelves under the bar. Cupboards fixed to the wall behind revealed a number of spirit bottles. A cupboard below turned out to be the door to a fridge containing additional spirits and soft drinks. Alongside the camouflaged fridge, a further cupboard revealed several cardboard cartons of a popular beer.

'Never worked in licensing,' said Cornell, 'but I suspect this set up is bordering on illegality.'

'I bet Bill Walton doesn't know about it,' suggested Marty Fielding.

There was a modern kitchen at the rear of the building with a window above the industrial size sink looking out on land that must also belong to the village hall. There were several picnic tables and a brick built barbecue on the roughly mown grass.

'Peter, set up a couple of tables with chairs,' directed Cornell. 'We'll use this place as a base instead of the pub. We can interview people here without the eagle eared Bill Walton listening in.'

'So,' mused Marty Fielding, 'this is where Stephanie Peston and her daughters met two years ago. They argued, the daughters left, but did their mother stay? Was she murdered here? And if so, why? Seems odd that when she was a kid, Stephanie was the most popular kid in the village, but as an adult someone chose to murder her.'

'That's if she was murdered, Marty. It's all supposition until we find out what happened to her. You got Peston's laptop?'

'Yes, sir. It's in my car.'

'Can you get it for Peter? He can have a look at it here. If he need's internet, he can go and use the pub's Wi-Fi. Anything in the solicitor's files of interest, Marty?'

'No, sir. Not a thing.'

'Sir,' said DC Ian Dennison phoning from the Newcastle incident room, 'just got back from the Donald Peston autopsy. Nothing we didn't know already, sir. Stabbed four times, twice in the heart. Died the evening before you found him. But...'

'But what, Ian?'

'Had a word with Tom Mawson, who was looking at documentation he found at Peston's home, sir.'

'And?'

'Peston had life insurance on Stephanie. A million quid, sir.'

Cornell allowed that to wash over him.

'Right, Ian. Are you managing OK?'

'Just had a knifing come in, sir, at a school in the West End.'

'Bloody hell. How old?'

'Wasn't a school kid, sir. It was a teacher. He thought two boys were dealing at the school gates. He went to investigate and one of them stuck him. He's in hospital undergoing surgery.'

'Does Chief Superintendent Blakeshaw want you on the case?'

'Not at the moment, sir. He's got uniform looking at it. Apparently the dealers, just two young lads, have been identified, so we probably won't be needed.'

'Fine. Keep things ticking over. I've a bobby sat outside Doctor Wainwright's room at the RVI. Can you check with him and make sure the change overs are going alright? The person who rang Wansbeck will not be aware of how much we know and until we release the fact we will be digging up the grave, may still be looking for her.'

Cornell closed the call and turned to DC Owusu.

'Peter, anything on that laptop?'

'Might be, sir. Peston kept a lot of notes about looking for Stephanie. Some look like reminders which he probably typed on his phone and synced to this laptop.'

'But it was the firm's laptop. It and he would be logged into the firm's network.'

'Not too difficult to get around that, sir, if you know the IP addresses. Probably used a dongle.'

'OK, before you blind me with science, what have you found?'

'Peston mentions in his notes that the villagers were very defensive when he asked about Stephanie. Only one person was helpful and that was James Dickinson. Peston discovered Dickinson knew Stephanie from their schooldays, in fact Dickinson admitted to him that he loved her, but she went out with and married Joseph Lockheed instead. Peston believed Dickinson was still in love with Stephanie and knew more about her recent disappearance than he was letting on. It seems Peston was trying to gain Dickinson's confidence by acting for him in a custody case, which Peston believed he had absolutely no chance of winning.'

'Good. We are building up quite a good picture of the disappearance and possible murder of Stephanie Woods. I hope if we solve that, it will lead us on to the killer of Dickinson and Peston.'

DOUGLAS JOHN KNOX

CHAPTER TWENTY EIGHT

DC Peter Owusu was pleased with himself for spotting the different qualities of the grass. He really didn't know how the others had missed it, but then again they weren't as good as he was at lateral thinking.

He recalled one day, someone brought a batch of those lateral thinking puzzles into work and while everyone else struggled with them over lunch, he had worked out all the answers correctly within minutes.

When he arrived at the scene of Doctor Wainwright's attack, he thought her discovery would not be on the gravestones. They had not been touched for years, so whatever she saw must have been on the ground. It may have been luck that he knelt down on Martin Brown's grave first, and the sun was shining, but he noticed immediately the slightly different shades of green reflecting in the sunlight. On closer inspection he saw that the grass in front of the gravestone was of a different texture and much finer than that of the rest.

Owusu had never been happier in his life as he was working in the murder investigation team. His boss treat him no differently to anyone else, which was a first in his police career. No longer did he get the shitty jobs; Cornell shared them out. No one called him Sambo, or Elmo or any other name ending in o. Tea making was shared out too, unlike his previous positions where the task was always undertaken by female and black staff.

He had not reverted to violence since his schooldays, but when PC John Wilson referred to his parents wearing grass skirts, he swung around and belted the speaker in the face, knocking him backwards into the table where the canteen of cutlery was placed for lunches, capsizing the knives and forks over the floor.

Owusu followed in after his blow and grabbed the front of Wilson's shirt.

'If I ever hear of you speaking of my parents like that again, I will take you down.'

Owusu left the canteen then, standing on Wilson's chest as he walked over him. Within minutes he was called to his sergeant's office.

'What happened?'

Owusu explained.

'Wilson says, it was you who hit him for no reason.'

'He's a liar. Why would I do that?'

'What do you want me to do Constable Owusu?'

'Nothing, sarge.'

'You don't want me to take it further?'

'No. He will have to explain the shiner. It's not my problem.'

'I'm surprised.'

'What you could do, sarge, is to get me transferred to CID. I'm wasted here.'

'Thanks very much, Peter. That really makes me feel great.'

'Sorry, sarge, but I would like to be a detective one day.'

'Leave it with me, son. I'll have a word.'

'So, PC Wilson,' said his sergeant, 'why should I not report you for racially abusing PC Owusu?'

'I didn't...'

'Don't give me that bullshit. I've been doing this job for a long time. Tell me again how PC Owusu suddenly said to himself, "I'm going to punch PC Wilson on the nose today, or maybe give him a black eye. I don't know why, I'll just do it for the hell of it." Your excuse is pathetic, can't you see that?'

'Sarge.'

'Right, here is what is going to happen. You go and get your eye checked out and then you get back to work. You dare go sick and I'll be straight upstairs with a racism charge. You will not miss a shift, do you hear me? And when people ask about your black eye, which is getting blacker by the minute, you will say, "I walked into a door." Do I make myself clear?'

TWO FEET UNDER

'Yes, sarge.'

Three weeks later PC Peter Owusu relinquished his uniform and joined the murder investigation team. Shortly after, Marty Fielding also joined, which for a while confused Owusu, as Fielding had been charged with racially abusing a black female constable and now he was going to be working alongside him.

He nonetheless greeted Fielding on his first day.

'Hiya, Marty. Good to have you with us,' he said.

'Yeah, good to be with you too,' Fielding responded with a knowing smile.

'That photograph you sent me of the grass, chief inspector,' said Tom Mawson telephoning Cornell from the Newcastle laboratory. 'Very expensive, hardwearing, fine grass, usually reserved for bowling greens and golf courses. Is there one of them near you?'

'There's a bowling green at the end of the village,' answered Cornell.

'I would check that out.'

'Thanks, Tom.'

Cornell closed the call.

'Peter, with me. Yes, Laura?' Cornell answered another call on his mobile.

'Sir, the first two people on Janet's list are being awkward. I suspect the others will be as well. We need a different strategy, like having something on them to talk about rather than whether they know anything.'

'You are quite right, Laura. Look, things are moving. I want a debrief first thing in the morning. You, Irene and Marty get your stuff together and go back to Newcastle now and for the rest of the afternoon do financials on those on Janet's list matching those who were standing around in the graveyard the other night.'

Cornell and Owusu were outside the bowling club, which was surrounded by a number of houses. The bowling green and clubhouse were enclosed by a white wicket fence. There was a gate which was locked, but climbing over it was not difficult. A noticeboard was fixed near the door of the clubhouse, one notice mentioning the groundsman, Nicolas Wordsworth. On another it mentioned the club secretary and while his address was given, there was no address for Wordsworth.

'Pity, that. I suppose we could knock on the secretary's door and ask,' said Cornell.

'I know a quicker way,' retorted Owusu. 'I bet the groundsman lives in one of these houses overlooking the green. If he does, you can be sure he is watching us at this very moment, waiting for us to put a foot on the green, his holy ground.'

It was on their return journey from the opposite corner of the green that an extremely irate, red faced individual materialised and challenged their parentage.

'You Nick Wordsworth?' asked Cornell.

'Get off my green! There's a match tonight, you ignorant bastards. Don't you know....'

Cornell now produced his warrant card.

'I asked if you were Nick Wordsworth.'

'What if I am?'

'We need to talk, Mr Wordsworth. I would like you to come to the village hall for a chat.'

'And you can bugger off. I'm not talking to any of you lot.'

'Is that because you don't like coppers, or you have something to hide?' challenged Cornell.

'For starters, I'm certainly not talking to the likes of him,' said Wordsworth, pointing at Owusu.

'Oh? And why not?' inquired Cornell.

'Do I have to spell it out?'

'DC Owusu, this man has racially abused you. What are you going to do about it?'

Owusu took out his handcuffs, grabbed Wordsworth's arm, expertly turned him around and applied the restraint to both wrists, while cautioning him under suspicion of murder.

'Will that do, sir?' Owusu asked when his charge was secured.

'That will do very nicely,' responded Cornell.

Wordsworth's expression had turned from one of aggression to absolute shock and horror, rendering him speechless. Owusu bundled him into the rear of the car.

In the meantime, Cornell looked around the perimeter of the clubhouse where he found nothing of interest. Off to one side there was a tool shed and to his surprise found the door unlocked.

At the rear of the shed, against the wall, stood a half full twenty five kilo bag of grass seed. The wording on the bag claimed that this was the finest, hardiest grass seed in the world and what it was suitable for. The stencilled words also listed the supplier, quantities and directions for application.

Wordsworth, having been removed from the car and released from the handcuffs, was seated opposite Cornell at a table in the village hall. Owusu was making three coffees from the machine in the kitchen. Wordsworth had not uttered a word since being cautioned.

TWO FEET UNDER

'This is a chat, Mr Wordsworth. It's informal. We don't have any recorders here, although DC Owusu will take notes. That's so we can follow up on what you say, not to incriminate you. You are entitled to a lawyer, but if you want one, we will have to go to the police station at Alnwick. Your choice.'

Wordsworth remained silent.

'Oh, the police station is also an option should you persist in muteness.'

'I can't help you,' mumbled Wordsworth, who obviously didn't want to go to Alnwick.

'Peter, the grass.'

Owusu placed the cellophane packet containing the blades of grass on the table.

'What is that?' asked Cornell.

'Looks like blades of grass to me,' replied Wordsworth.

'And you are correct, Mr Wordsworth. But they are no ordinary blades of grass, are they? They are very special blades of grass, a variety exclusive to bowling greens and golf courses. Far too expensive for the general public.'

Wordsworth merely shrugged his shoulders as if to say, so what?

'You see, Mr Wordsworth, this very same grass was taken from the grave of a Mr Martin Brown, who died in 1931. It had been re-sown, I would guess about two years ago. Why do you think that was?'

At which point Wordsworth turned a pale shade of grey. He swallowed, trying to rehydrate his dry mouth.

'Would you have an explanation for that, Mr Wordsworth?' asked Peter Owusu, sitting at the next table.

The interviewee did not respond.

'Let me tell you what I think happened,' explained Cornell. 'Stephanie Lockheed, a native of this village, having left under a bit of a cloud twenty odd years before, returned two years ago. We do know she visited the village hall on the Saturday evening, then she disappeared off the face the earth again after only being here a couple of days. She's never been traced and I think the reason for that is she died here, possibly murdered. Neither she, nor her body has ever been found, perhaps because it's buried in the grave of Martin Brown. How did I do?'

Nicolas Wordsworth sat slumped in his chair, looking as if a large amount of blood had been drained from his body.

'You've got nothing on me,' Wordsworth uttered finally after a long pause.

He was right of course, the police officers had nothing on him. Having a sack of specialist seed in his possession of the type used to re-sow the surface of a suspicious grave, without an admission, was next to nothing.

'You can go, Mr Wordsworth, but please be aware you are a person of interest to us. We will probably need to interview you again. DC Owusu, show Mr Wordsworth out.'

Wordsworth almost ran from the village hall.

'Do you think he's the murderer, sir?' asked DC Owusu.

'I think he supplied the grass seed to cover the grave when it had been refilled after Stephanie's body was put in it. He may have a motive for her murder, but I cannot see it at the moment. I certainly don't think he murdered either Dickinson or Peston. On the other hand, Stephanie Peston, or Lockheed, nee Woods, may not be dead at all and living it up in a villa on the Algarve.'

CHAPTER TWENTY NINE

DCI Max Cornell parked illegally in the grounds of the Royal Victoria Infirmary, Newcastle. He had tried the hospital's car parks, but they were all full. He could have parked outside the hospital, but why should he? If challenged, he would argue he was here on official business and in some respects he was.

He wished he had one of those magnetic blue lights the American plain clothes cops used for emergencies.

He was late for visiting but he assumed Marian and his mother would be there. He was right and his spirits lifted when he saw Mabel Wainwright wide awake and propped up in bed in a sitting position. Some of the tubes were still in place and the bruising around her throat still very much in evidence.

She was still unable or not allowed to speak, but she had a note pad and pencil in front of her.

She opened her arms for him and his mother got up to make room.

'Mabel thought you weren't coming,' said his mother as Max was held in a vice like grip for a few moments.

'Got held up,' he responded.

'Isn't Mum looking great, Max?' said Marian enthusiastically.

No, she is not, thought Max. *She looks terrible.*

'Yeah,' he said, 'she's looking fine,' he lied.

'Hopefully, she'll be able to talk soon,' continued Marian.

Mabel shook her head as if to suggest she wouldn't.

'Oh yes you will,' returned Marian.

'Let's not get into panto mode,' offered Max, who turned towards his mother. 'How's my dog?'

'Your dog is fine. He and Annie were actually playing together this morning.'

'It was so funny,' interjected Marian. 'Rex was …….'

Mabel tapped her notepad vigorously to get attention.

'*Hey, this visit is about me!!!!*' she wrote.

'Of course,' said Max. 'Let's be serious. Mabel, did you see who attacked you?'

She scribbled on her pad and showed it to Max, shaking her head slightly.

'*Only glimpse, grabbed from behind.*'

'Male or female?'

This time she thought for a moment, then scribbled.

'*Not sure strong wore man hat but smelt fancy soap.*'

'A woman?' asked Max.

Mabel wrote, *'possibly.'*

'What did you see that prompted you to call me, Mabel?'

'Martin Brown grave not right,' the doctor wrote.

'And you know that because the grass on the grave didn't match the surrounding grass.'

Mabel smiled and wrote, *'clever clogs.'*

'We are waiting for a court order to open the grave. Expect to find Stephanie Peston in it. If we don't, I'm directing traffic from next Monday.'

'I didn't think they did that anymore,' said Max's mother.

'I think they would create a vacancy especially for me.'

Just then a bell rang to signify that visiting time was over. Mabel squeezed Max's hand and wrote, *'too short'* on her pad.

He nodded and as he kissed her forehead he whispered, 'love you.'

'I know' she wrote on her pad to show him.

Back in his Cullercoats home, reunited if only temporarily with his beloved German Shepherd, Max opened a can of beer and sat back in his favourite chair with his feet on a pouffe. He took a long drink from the can, switched on the television and decided he wouldn't think about work.

Using the remote, he surfed for football; there wasn't any as it was another three weeks to the start of the season. The cricket test match had only lasted three days and he didn't want to watch highlights of England losing. Wimbledon was finished. There was a repeat boxing match between two middleweights from the seventies and an American football game, which he didn't understand. He switched the TV off in disgust.

'What should we do, Rex old son?' he called to his dog.

The German Shepherd had been chewing on something Marian had given him and on hearing his master's voice sat up with a huge red rubber bone in his mouth.

'You look ridiculous,' said Max.

The dog walked over to his master and dropped the rubber bone in his lap. 'I think you are bored too. Come on, let's go for walk. Go get your leash.'

The dog set off into the hallway, reached up to take his leash from a coat hook and dragged it into the lounge.

The sun had lost some of its heat and was gradually losing height, but it was still warm and the forecast was good for tomorrow. Cullercoats was full of people out walking and enjoying the warm evening.

As they walked down the steps on to Whitley Bay beach, Max let the dog off the leash. It was a purposeful action in order to see who was driving the car that had been following him for most of the day.

The vehicle was a Nissan Qashqai. Both the driver and front seat passenger were wearing baseball hats and could have been either male or female. *Could it be Amy Carter and Todd? If it were, what was in their minds?*

Rex, once he was free of his leash, set off at break neck speed into the distance, sometimes creating a path through beach goers, who wisely gave space to the big dog. Mabel thought Rex was a throwback to when dogs were wolves. Maybe she was right, he was big enough, probably bigger than most wolves. In a matter of minutes, he was on the return journey creating a similar path.

It was almost dark when the two returned home. Max had another beer then went to bed.

Sometime during the night Max was awoken by a noise. He couldn't place the sound other than it seemed to be from downstairs.

Could it be Rex? He heard the noise again. *What the hell was that.* Rex didn't usually move around at night.

He was about to get out of bed and investigate when a figure appeared at the bedroom door. It was Amy and she was armed with an automatic pistol. She signalled with the Glock for him to stay where he was.

Where the hell was Rex? Come on, boy. Save me.

The thought occurred to Max that Amy had killed the dog.

'What the hell do you want, Amy?' he asked gruffly.

'You insulted me.'

'No, I didn't.'

'You turned your back on me and your son.'

'Todd is not my son and by all accounts, not Jim Carter's either. You must have put yourself about a bit back then, Amy.'

Amy Carter pulled her face into a snarl.

'That's not the point,' she said.

'It is the point. What the hell are you doing here?'

Amy fired. The bullet missed Max's head by inches. The miss must have been deliberate. Amy was an expert shot with a handgun, better than Max.

'I need money for Todd,' she said.

'Well you are not getting it from me,' he replied.

Amy fired again, this time hitting Max in the left shoulder. The force of the bullet pinning him back against the headboard. He placed his right hand over the bullet wound to stem the flow of blood. Then Amy fired again, hitting Max in the right shoulder. He was beyond trying to stop the bleeding and now there was no pain, only numbness.

'If you kill me, Amy, you are still not going to get any money,' he struggled to say.

He looked up at Amy, her mouth so twisted, she was showing her teeth. Max watched in amazement as her canine teeth grew and her face began growing hair. Her chin taking on the shape of a wolf's. She looked like Rex. Max screamed, his arms useless. He had no way of lifting himself off the bed. He was about to roll off, when Amy, now fully transformed into a two legged wolf, fired into his forehead at point blank range.

Max awoke in a sweat. He felt his shoulders for bullet holes and blood and was relieved there were none. He switched on his bedside lamp. Rex had come upstairs and was standing next to the bed, obviously bewildered by his master's screaming, but slowly wagging his tail when he saw Max was OK.

Max reached out and scratched the dog's head.

'It's alright, lad. I'm alright,' he said assuredly, running through the nightmare in his mind.

The dog was not reassured and put its mighty right paw on Max's naked chest, whereupon Max decided it was time to get up. He looked at his watch and the time was five thirty a.m. Outside it was light. He would make a good old fashioned English breakfast to start the day off.

'Come on, lad. Downstairs.'

The big dog set off down to the kitchen where he spent his night's. He sat in his large bed waiting for the next instalment of his life. To assuage his guilt at eating, Max threw the dog a couple of dog biscuits which he collected and placed in his bed. He would lie down and eat them later at his leisure.

CHAPTER THIRTY

DCI Max Cornell and the chief superintendent sat at the back of the incident room while Sergeant Donaldson stood like a school teacher at the front of the class. She was alongside the whiteboard and a flipchart and asking questions of the team, which had that morning been increased by one with the return of David Watkins.

'You are on paternity leave, David,' Donaldson had stated.

'Please give me a break, sarge. Her mother, my mother, her grandmother and our next door neighbour are all playing pass the parcel with the baby. Each waiting for her to start crying, then like athletes at the start of a race waiting for the gun, fight over her for who can pick her up and show who is best at stopping her crying. I can't stand it anymore. If I didn't get out, I'd go crazy. Please, sarge.'

'David, you need to assert your authority,' responded Donaldson.

'I will tonight,' he replied somewhat pathetically.

Donaldson continued with her brainstorming but bestowing a, "no you won't," expression.

'What information do we need to progress the enquiry? Marty, you start.'

Donaldson involved all the team, asking her questions of one then another, accepting all the answers regardless of their quality.

'She's good,' whispered the superintendent.

'Yes, she is,' responded Cornell.

'I would watch my back if I were you, chief inspector.'

'I'd be more worried if I were you, sir.'

The chief superintendent merely nodded, seemingly not doubting Cornell's prediction of Donaldson's rise to the top, rather, paying attention to a memo his personal assistant who had entered the room, had just given him.

The sergeant eventually asked Cornell if he wished to contribute. He stood up and walked to the front.

'So, we all think Stephanie Peston is the key to the murders.'

'And I have the court order to open that grave,' said the chief superintendent from the rear. 'First thing tomorrow, chief inspector?'

'Yes, sir,' replied Cornell.

'Good, I'll arrange for a digger to be on site.'

The chief superintendent left the room.

Irene Stainton lifted her hand for attention.

'Sir, I've been thinking about a connection between the deaths of James Dickinson and Stephanie Peston.'

'Yes, Irene?'

'Well, we are wondering why Dickinson was in the graveyard the evening he was murdered. Could he have been at the grave of this guy Brown? I mean, if Stephanie is buried there, it may have been him who put the flowers on the grave.'

'And someone didn't want him doing that because it was drawing attention. Is that what you are suggesting?' asked Cornell.

'It's a possibility, sir.'

'Ian and David. Anything on the financial checks?'

'Only that some on Janet's list deposit cash on a regular basis, as do a couple who were in the graveyard when Doctor Mabel was injured.'

'Listen up everyone. I want all those on both Janet Beveridge's list and Irene's photograph interviewed under caution this afternoon in the village hall. I want explanations for the cash deposits. Peter, you seek out a recording machine. And this is important. Do not mention anything about the grave being opened to anyone.'

The drive north was uneventful. Cornell drove by himself with his dog in the passenger seat, the rest of the team in two cars, one driven by Fielding, the other by Donaldson. They parked at the *Sword and Lance* in East Hewick. Bill Walton's face lit up as the team entered his establishment carrying their overnight bags.

'Welcome back. I've missed you all. What is that?' suddenly spotting Rex.

'That's my dog. He's a German Shepherd,' answered Cornell.

'He may have been once. Is he staying with us? I had to let the cage go.'

'Yes, he's staying. He's harmless unless you don't feed him. Bill, I have a couple of cans of dog meat with me, can I put them in your fridge?'

'I suppose so. Is chicken and chips with peas OK for tonight's meal? I promise not to mix it up with the dog food.'

'Yes, that will do,' Cornell answered for all. 'Bill, take a look at this photo and see if you can identify any of the people on it.'

Irene Stainton showed the landlord the photo on her phone. He was able to identify all but two of the bystanders, they not having frequented his establishment. DC Stainton wrote down their names.

Cornell recognised Gladys Hume, the vicar and his wife and Nicolas Wordsworth of the seven men and women at the graveyard who looked on as Mabel Wainwright was being cared for.

There was also something about the photograph of seven people that niggled at Cornell.

He stared at it for a long time, but whatever it was didn't jump out at him.

Cornell's mobile rang.

'Sir,' said Ian Dennison.

'Yes, Ian?'

'Someone tried to gain access to Doctor Wainwright's room this morning, and it wasn't the press.'

'Bloody hell!' exclaimed Cornell standing.

'Don't worry, sir, whoever it was didn't get very far.'

'Man or woman?' asked Cornell.

'That's the strange thing, sir. The uniform wasn't sure.'

'He wasn't sure?' Cornell repeated. 'Doesn't he know the difference?'

'He said the person was tall, sir. Dressed in trousers and a jacket, looked like a man from behind, but walked like a woman.'

'That's great.' Then he remembered Mabel thought the same. 'So what happened?'

'The uniform said that when the person saw him, he/she about turned and left the hospital in quick time. The guard didn't want to leave his post, so didn't follow him/her.'

'OK, thank the officer for me, Ian.'

TWO FEET UNDER

CHAPTER THIRTY ONE

While his officers were interviewing the villagers who were both on Janet Beveridge's list and in DC Stainton's photograph, Cornell, with Rex as his front seat passenger, re-visited the Lockheed farm. He was interested to know what the farmer thought of Stephanie being murdered and buried in the graveyard.

Cornell felt sure the murderers of Stephanie Peston, James Dickinson and Donald Peston were one and the same, but it was not Joseph Lockheed. The farmer had no motive for killing Stephanie twenty five years after their divorce. He may have had motive for Dickinson's murder, but if he did, Cornell doubted he would have stabbed Dickinson several times and left him in the graveyard. As far as Donald Peston goes, Lockheed had probably never heard of him.

Cornell found Lockheed with farm hand Harry Jamieson in the farmyard trying to secure a cantankerous Highland bull to an iron ring set in the wall of a building. They were using a rope tied both around the animal's neck and to the ring in its nose, but the bull had other ideas about being secured and was not cooperating. Cornell refrained from assisting and remained in his vehicle. Eventually the men, at great risk from the animal's huge and treacherous needle sharp horns, managed to fasten the rope to the ring in the wall, at which point Cornell lowered the passenger window for Rex's benefit and got out of his car. However, he couldn't fail to notice the life size model of the rear end of a cow alongside.

'Afternoon, chief inspector,' greeted Lockheed, while straightening his dishevelled clothing. 'Lovely day, isn't it?' he shouted above the bellowing of the bull and added, 'to what do we owe the pleasure?'

Cornell decided he would keep his distance from the bellowing animal which was pawing the ground and kicking out with his back feet while trying to pull the iron ring it was attached to, out of the wall.

'Mr Lockheed how would you react if I told you I think your first wife Stephanie is buried here in East Hewick, in the graveyard?'

The farmer paused for a second or two, clearly shocked at the submission.

'I wasn't aware that she had died, but if she has and was buried here, I'm sure I would have known about it. So would my daughter, Lesley. What are you getting at, chief inspector?'

'I don't think Stephanie left the village two years ago when she disappeared within two days of returning. It's possible she was killed and buried here.'

'That's some theory, chief inspector. You don't think I did it, do you?'

'Do you ever go to the village hall Saturday night dance, Mr Lockheed?'

'Been once many years ago when I was fourteen or fifteen. Decided then it was not my scene. Too "churchie" for me. Since then, I've only been in the village hall once; to a wedding reception for my cousin. Why do you ask, chief inspector?'

'I think Stephanie attended the village hall on the Saturday night of her visit two years ago. Your twin daughters did too, to see their mother, but the meeting didn't go well. Your daughters left and later in the evening something bad happened to Stephanie.'

'Well, whatever it was, it sure as hell wasn't me who did it.'

'Did you know the pathologist was attacked in the graveyard the other evening?' asked Cornell.

'Bloody hell! No, I did not, chief inspector and before you ask, I was over in Carlisle on business, Saturday and Sunday. Got back last night.'

'Thought you ought to know, Mr Lockheed, we are opening a grave tomorrow morning and I expect to find Stephanie's remains there.'

'Whose grave?'

'A chap called Brown, but I don't think that matters. Any grave would have done.'

'Well I never. Should I tell Lesley?'

'Might be a good idea if you kept it to yourself until we've opened the grave tomorrow morning, Mr Lockheed.'

'Right, I'll do that. But you've not answered my question. Am I still under suspicion?'

'Surprising how many villagers have told me you are the villain here, Mr Lockheed, but none of them have any proof, only talk. However, until I find the killer everyone is under suspicion, but I'm not arresting you today.'

'I'll take that as a probably not, then.'

'Mr Lockheed, may I ask you a question?'

'Certainly, fire away,' returned the farmer.

'What on earth are you doing with this poor bull?'

'I'm waiting for the vet, chief inspector. He is going to take some semen from William Wallace here.'

Cornell looked at William Wallace. The bull was like a huge shaggy teddy bear, its eyesight surely impaired by the amount of thick hair hanging over its face.

'I thought you only dealt in Jersey cattle, Mr Lockheed.'

'I have a small herd of Highland cattle which spend most of their time in the hills, but every now and again, William Wallace has to come down here and perform.'

'I'm surprised he still has his horns, formidable as they are.'

'They add to his prowess, chief inspector. Makes his semen more saleable when customers see him, or a photograph of him.'

Cornell now turned his attention to the fake cow, but before he asked the question, he suddenly understood.

'Fine, I don't want to know anymore. I'll go now before the vet arrives. I wouldn't want to embarrass William.'

Cornell returned to his car and got in beside Rex. After raising the passenger window, they set off out of the farmyard along the same road where not so many days before, James Dickinson and his followers were protesting.

A van advertising a veterinary practice came towards him and Cornell drove on to the grass verge to let it past, the occupant acknowledging his courteous action with a wave. Then a Nissan Qashqai turned on to the road and drove slowly towards him.

Cornell stopped his car and switched off the engine. The appearance of the Qashqai did not surprise him. Several times that afternoon he had spotted the vehicle in his rear view mirror whilst driving to East Hewick.

It was time to sort Amy's problem out once and for all.

Cornell told his dog to stay and he reopened the passenger window for air to circulate in the car on this very hot day. Two occupants emerged from the Qashqai, Amy and Todd Carter, both expressionless, Todd standing almost a foot taller than his mother.

'You never were much good at following anybody, Amy,' said Cornell walking towards his ex-girlfriend and her son. 'So, tell me what you want.'

Todd Carter suddenly took a step forward surprisingly quick for such a big boy and catching Cornell unawares, punched him squarely on the chin. The blow knocked Cornell backwards a few steps before he fell against the bonnet of his vehicle and ended up on the ground next to his right front wheel.

Rex went apoplectic seeing his master being attacked and somehow managed to liberate himself from his seatbelt and squeeze out of the car through the passenger window, barking loudly.

This concerned Cornell as he lay on the ground. Amy may have a gun and would not hesitate to shoot the dog, but before he could be stopped, the big German Shepherd flew at Todd Carter. The weight of dog sent the youth backwards and on to the ground where Rex sank his teeth into Todd's right arm, much as a trained police dog would do. Todd screamed.

Cornell was impressed. Rex had never had any police training, but Todd had his right arm out in front of him so it was only natural the dog would grab the nearest appendage.

Cornell got to his feet and grabbing the dog's collar tried to drag him off the youth. Amy was yelling threats and brandishing an automatic pistol. Suddenly there were shouts from the farm.

Amy's eyes widened and Cornell followed her gaze to see the Highland bull no longer roped to a steel ring attached to a building wall in the farm yard, but galloping towards them at great speed, the steel ring bouncing along behind him creating sparks at every encounter with the road.

There were cries of, 'Look out!,' from farmer Lockheed and Harry Jamieson, who were chasing after the bull at a run, but losing the race.

Cornell finally managed to extricate Rex from Todd and held him behind the car so he would not run in front of the bull. Todd Carter was still on the ground nursing his damaged arm, but off the road. Amy Carter seemed to be frozen in time as William Wallace, at full pace, speared her through the abdomen with his left horn,. Cornell winced as he saw the bloodied tip of the horn emerge from Amy's back.

Her blood curdling scream echoed in Cornell's head as the bull, now attempting to remove the impaled object, flung Amy one way and then the other, her blood spattering everything within a twelve foot radius.

Holding on to Rex's collar, Cornell watched the terrible scene in horror, yet unable to do anything. Amy Carter had ceased screaming and her arms flailed uncontrollably, suggesting she was either unconscious, or already dead.

Lockheed and Jamieson arrived just as William Wallace, using its front feet, managed to extricate Amy from its impressive crown. Jamieson, meanwhile, managed to loop a rope around the bull's back legs and with Lockheed's assistance, toppled the bull on to its side. Another farm hand and the vet arrived with more ropes to secure the bull, and a powerful sedative that had the escapee animal snoring within minutes.

Todd Carter, crying pitifully, not at his damaged arm, but at the broken body of his mother, whom he held and rocked gently in his arms. Cornell made him stop while he checked Amy's pulse. There was nothing. He decided to leave the boy nursing the body. Rex stood nearby panting in the heat of the day, but ready to pounce in an instant on the person who had attacked his master.

TWO FEET UNDER

Cornell rang the Alnwick police station and asked for Inspector Stewart.

'Mary, it's Max Cornell here. I'm at Lockheed's farm outside East Hewick. I have a death here, a bizarre accident and nothing to do with the East Hewick murders. I need you and an ambulance here ASAP.'

'I can be there in half an hour, sir, but I've a car out near you; I'll see if it's available.'

Within ten minutes a police vehicle turned on to the farm road. Two officers alighted; Cornell recognised one as PC Green. They walked over to where Amy Carter lay with her son draped around her.

'There's a Glock pistol over there on the grass,' said Cornell pointing. 'I haven't touched it.'

Todd Carter lashed out at the two officers as they tried to pull him away from his mother. That precipitated him being thrown to the ground and handcuffed. He continued to wail.

'DCI Cornell,' probed Green, 'have you tried CPR on the victim, sir?'

'No, I think she's quite dead, PC Green. I'd be surprised if she wasn't. She was impaled on one of these beauties.'

Cornell touched the end of the bull's left horn. Amy's blood covered it from the tip all the way to the head.

'What went on here, sir?'

'This bull escaped from the farm and attacked the lady.'

'May I ask what you were all doing here, sir?' questioned the other officer.

Cornell despite his rank and the need to be elsewhere, knew he couldn't just walk away from this scene. The two police officers had been deployed and were doing their job.

'I'm investigating a murder that PC Green is aware of. This incident has nothing to do with that. This lady is called Amy Carter. She is an ex-girlfriend of mine who has lived in America for fifteen years. This is her son, Todd Carter, who was about to go to university in the States to study basketball. Don't ask. Amy wanted me to pay for it as it was understood until six months ago, that I was his father. I refused, so she came to the UK to kill me.'

'Is that why there is a Glock automatic here, sir?'

'Yes, it belongs to the lady.'

The officer had picked up the weapon and placed it in an evidence bag. At the same time, he looked questioningly at Cornell, not at all sure of his explanation.

A siren was heard in the distance. Ambulance: Cornell could tell the difference now.

'Sir, is Inspector Stewart aware of this accident?' asked PC Green.

'Yes, she advised me that you were nearby and that you would respond.'

'What about statements, sir?'

'I'll sort that out with Inspector Stewart.'

It was clear that the two officers were not happy with the situation but were content to leave it to their superior.

The ambulance arrived and two paramedics jumped out.

'What have we got?' one asked.

'Dead female,' PC Green stated.

'Christ, what happened to her?' the paramedic asked on taking a closer look at the mutilated body.

'Appears she had an encounter with this bull,' replied PC Green.

Inspector Mary Stewart arrived with another officer. She looked at the body and was clearly repulsed by the scene. She ambled over to where Cornell and his dog were standing.

'You're not helping the Northumbrian tourist industry very much, sir.'

'Oh, I don't know, inspector. I can see droves of people coming here now out of curiosity.'

Cornell described his relationship with Amy Carter and her son. He explained their separation fifteen years ago and her visit to the UK six months prior, the email requests for funds and Jim Carter's phone call.

'Do you still have the emails, sir?' Mary Stewart asked.

'I do and I can give you a statement with regard to everything else in due course, but I have murders and a team of detectives to see to at this moment.'

'I understand, sir. What do we do with the son?'

'Well, I'm not sure he has committed an offence. I think he was totally influenced by his mother who lost her way these last few months. He could probably do with some counselling, but my advice would be to put him on the first plane back to the States. I have his stepfather's mobile number. Not sure about their relationship.'

Their conversation was interrupted by James Lockheed who was arranging for the transportation of his bull back to the farm. Meanwhile, the paramedics had loaded the body of Amy Carter into the ambulance.

'How will this affect me?' asked Lockheed.

'Well, we can't charge the bull with murder, Mr Lockheed, but I'm afraid you may be held responsible for the death of the lady. Inspector Stewart will need a statement from you regarding the bull's escape and she will discuss the matter with the CPS. It's up to them as to what to charge you with.'

'Thank you. Christ, if it's not one thing it's another. Did you know who the lady was?'

'I did as a matter of fact, but it's a long story.'

'Will the press get hold of it?'

'Inevitably. By the way, did William Wallace produce before leaving home?'

'No. He went berserk when the vet arrived. He pulled the ring out of the wall and took off.' Lockheed walked off a couple of steps then turned back. 'You seem quite indifferent to this incident, chief inspector.'

'One of those things,' Cornell lied. He was inwardly rejoicing that he no longer had Amy Carter to worry about.

CHAPTER THIRTY TWO

'What on earth happened to you, sir?' asked Laura Donaldson, observing Cornell's blood spattered clothing as he entered the village pub.

'This is getting to be a habit with you lot,' said Bill Walton.

'It's been a long day already so I'll tell you tonight. You probably won't believe it. How have we got on with the interviews?'

'Hard work, sir. We've seen Gladys Hume, a John Soulsby, Edward Smith and Nicolas Wordsworth. Apart from Gladys, they remembered Stephanie turning up at the village hall a couple of years ago, but nothing happened. I'm not sure I believe them. Gladys couldn't, or wouldn't recall anything. I would have liked to have told them about the opening of Brown's grave tomorrow. I think that may have stimulated some answers.'

'I realise that Laura, but the murderer may go on the run if we release that information. That's it for today. I need a shower and a change of clothing.'

Later, after the team had had their evening meal, Cornell explained his afternoon's exploits with the farmer, the bull and Amy Carter. Then using the table usually reserved during the lunch time for the domino players, he set about writing a statement regarding that incident. He was using Irene Stanton's laptop and when he had finished, he emailed his statement to Mary Stewart, promising to call in at the station to verify it. He then uploaded the photo of the villagers from Stainton's mobile phone so he could look at it in greater detail.

Something in the photo had bothered him. He was missing something. What the hell was it? Then he remembered the evidence. Of course! Viewing the photograph on a laptop rather than a smart phone made things easier and zooming in and out over every individual in the photo, he found it. The clue. That one piece of information that solves the crime. The killer wouldn't have even thought about it. But there it was, now that it was large enough to see, staring him right in the face.

Should he tell his team? They were in the middle of a pool tournament organised by Marty Fielding who had threatened revenge at Irene Stainton who had seven balled him during a previous match. No, they were enjoying themselves. He would tell them in the morning.

His mother and Marian would have returned from the hospital by now. He rang his mother.

'Mabel is much improved, Max. All the tubes and stuff have been taken away and she is able to eat small amounts of mashed up food. However...'

'There's always a but, isn't there?'

'The doctors are worried about her voice, Max. She should have been able to speak by now. She tries, but nothing comes out. She is very frustrated.'

'I don't blame her. How's Marian?' he asked.

'Trying to look on the bright side. But she's understandably concerned for her mother, and she's also missing Rex. My little dog is not an alternative, although Marian is doing her best to entertain her.'

'I can see it's going to be a problem with Rex when Mabel comes out of hospital and we all go back to normality.'

'Well, I can see an easy solution to that problem and if you took some time to think about it, you would too. Bye.'

Cornell killed the call. His mother wouldn't let up on him having a partner, would she?

There had been a missed call from Mary Stewart. He rang her.

'Sir, I've got your statement. Thanks. Just had the lab on the phone. They observed a smell of alcohol when they took Mrs Carter's body out of the body bag. The blood test will confirm, but they say it's very possible she shouldn't have been driving.'

'How's Todd?'

'He's with one of my officer's; Sally Peabody. She's a very good listener, has a degree in psychology or something like that. We've been in touch with the boy's step father, Jim Carter, too. He is coming over to collect him.'

'That's good of him, especially when he's not a blood relative.'

'Feels he has an obligation to the boy, he's still his stepfather.'

'Wish the lad all the best from me, would you?'

'Yes, sir. Carter is arranging for his wife's body to be taken to the States as well. '

'I'm pleased about that. I had a thought her burial might have fallen to me. Right, Mary, I want you, some officers and the custody van in East Hewick tomorrow morning. Nineish will do. Can you do that?'

'Certainly. Sounds like you've cracked the murder, sir.'

'Almost there, Mary, almost there.'

Cornell moved over to the pool table where DC Stainton was about to pot the black and thus win the final and £5 prize money, the landlord having donated the extra pound. DC Fielding, the losing finalist offered his hand to shake.

'All right if my dog stays in the bar overnight, Bill?' asked Cornell of the host.

'No problem. I will sleep soundly in the knowledge that any would be burglar would be torn to shreds.'

'Christ, don't you think I've had enough of that for one day?' answered Cornell.

TWO FEET UNDER

CHAPTER THIRTY THREE

'What?' snapped the voice on the phone.
'Ethel's just called. She says there are police cars and a digger at the church.'
'So?'
'What are you going to do about it?'
'What do you mean, what am I going to do about it?'
'Well you got us into this mess.'
'Oh, just a minute. I'll have a word with the chief inspector and ask him if he'll stop the investigation.'
'Hey, I didn't do anything. It was you who.....' but the phone line had gone dead.

Nicolas Wordsworth put the receiver back in its cradle. He was worried. He didn't know why he'd made the phone call now that he thought about it. What did he expect? He wished he'd never gone to the village hall dances on a Saturday night. They weren't that good anyway. Dancing to the same old records, week after week, month after month. The night Stephanie Lockheed turned up drunk after a space of twenty five years was a bit of excitement, at least early on in the evening. It got a bit nasty later.

Emily Wordsworth had never gone to the dances. She couldn't dance. The polio she endured as a child had left her with a permanent limp and an inability to pronounce certain words properly. She didn't want to embarrass her husband.

She would have preferred it if he hadn't gone out on a Saturday night. She was lonely sitting in on her own watching game shows and Casualty. Then there was that Saturday two years ago when he didn't come home until after two the following morning.

He refused to say where he'd been. He'd been very aggressive towards her. "None of her damned business," he'd said. She thought he must have been seeing another woman, she was nothing special after all. She cooked his meals, cleaned his house, washed his clothes, but he probably wanted more than she was giving him. Then she found the soil on his suit. Now where had that come from?

Their relationship never improved. There was something wrong, something kept occurring that put Nicolas into a bad mood and Emily knew whatever it was emanated from that Saturday night. His temper grew worse, he snapped at people. Had he not been an excellent groundsman, he may well have lost his job at the bowls club. Several members, she knew, had complained of his behaviour.

And now this morning he was very agitated, ever since Ethel Cartwright had phoned. Emily had answered the call and sensed Ethel was unsettled too.

TWO FEET UNDER

Nicolas made a call afterwards. Emily overheard but could make little out of the conversation other than police cars, diggers and mess. Was her husband in trouble? Had whatever happened two years ago come back to haunt him?

'I have to go out,' he said, grabbing a jacket from a hook on the back of the door.

'Will you be long?' she asked, not pronouncing her L's.

He ignored her and walked down the path to the gate. He turned, was about to say something, but decided not to and carried on walking.

Emily ambled to the gate to watch her husband march towards the home of Ethel Cartwright and her mother. As he was almost at Ethel's gate, a police car drove up and stopped at her house. Two uniformed male officers got out. Nicolas stopped walking and stood by the car. One officer began talking to him and after a few minutes turned him around and handcuffed him. The other officer had gone into the home of Ethel Cartwright.

Emily turned and walked back inside. She knew she would not see Nicolas for a while and didn't feel too badly about it.

CHAPTER THIRTY FOUR

The mini digger was driven off the trailer by the owner of Parkinson's Plant Hire, Paul Parkinson himself. Apparently, his usual digger driver had refused to have anything to do with opening a grave.

Marty Fielding and Peter Owusu directed the digger into the graveyard and on towards the grave of Martin Brown.

Already a small group of onlookers had assembled, their curiosity or fear having been aroused by the arrival of the digger, two police cars and a police van.

But not the murderer, Cornell observed. The coroner stood alongside Inspector Mary Stewart and Tom Mawson, who was supervising the digger which had begun to remove the top layer of expensive, fine grass.

'Inspector Stewart,' directed Cornell. 'The residents on Irene's photograph and Janet Beveridge's list, I want those arrested. Will you and your officers do that for me? Sergeant Donaldson, you carry on here. Let me know the moment you find anything, which I'm sure you will. DC's Fielding and Stainton, come with me.'

'Where are we going, sir?' asked Marty Fielding.

'To arrest a murderer, detective constable, and you can do the honours.'

The trio walked along the pathway to the rectory. At the front door, Cornell rang the bell, Fielding and Stainton unsure of what exactly was going on. The door was opened by the Reverend Neville Mason, dressed in a suit for travelling. His wife Mavis, similarly attired stood behind him. Two suitcases could be seen further along the passage.

'Going somewhere, Reverend?' asked Cornell.

'I, I, I......,' he stuttered.

'Thought as much. How about you Mavis? You going with him?'

The vicar's wife stood stony faced and remained silent.

'May we come in?' asked Cornell, but without waiting for an answer pushed his way past the vicar. Fielding and Stainton followed.

Cornell grabbed the right arm of the vicar's wife and pulled up her sleeve. Left handed people usually wear watches on the right wrist and Mavis Mason was no exception. She tried to resist but Cornell was able to point to the white band of skin where a watch strap used to be.

'Not wearing a watch today, Mavis? You weren't wearing one when the photo was taken of you with the group of bystanders the other night either. Did the strap break in your struggle with James when you murdered him?'

Mavis Mason said nothing, her poker face showing absolutely no emotion. However, the Reverend Neville Mason had slumped into a chair alongside a grandfather clock and he had his head in his hands.

'DC Stainton, ring the lab and arrange for a forensics team to go over the rectory with a fine tooth comb. DC Fielding, arrest Mrs Mavis Mason on suspicion of murder and the vicar as an accessory.'

As Fielding was reciting the cautions, Cornell rang Ian Dennison at Newcastle incident room and requested he do a financial check on the Mason's bank accounts.

Sergeant Donaldson entered the hallway.

'Sir, we've found a body in the grave. Just two feet under.'

'That's a relief. We are charging Mrs Mason here with the murder of James Dickinson and Donald Peston and, not least, the attempted murder of Mabel Wainwright, the latter on two occasions; once in the graveyard and the other yesterday at the RVI.'

There was a flicker of disclosure from the vicar's wife. 'You didn't think I knew about that, did you, Mrs Mason?'

'Sir,' added Donaldson, 'there was a handbag buried with the body. The contents are well preserved. There are credit cards in the name of Mrs S Peston.'

'Good, that suggests it is indeed the body of Stephanie.'

Cornell turned to the vicar's wife. 'I suspect we will be adding the murder of Stephanie Peston to the list as well. I hope you have not started watching any new serials on the tele, Mavis.'

The vicar's wife remained silent as Irene Stainton applied handcuffs. When she patted Mavis down, a large, folded knife was found in her jacket pocket. Holding it by only two fingers Stainton handed the knife to Cornell, who held open an evidence bag for her to drop it into. 'Even found the murder weapon too.'

Marty Fielding was trying to get the vicar to stand up so he could apply handcuffs to him too.

'Don't bother cuffing him, DC Fielding. The reverend isn't going to run. Instead he's going to travel back with me to Newcastle and during the journey he is going to tell me everything. Isn't that right, vicar?'

Cornell helped the vicar, who seemed to have lost the full use of his limbs, out of the chair. Marty Fielding assisted.

'Walk him outside while I get my car. When you get back to Newcastle, DC Fielding, you and DC Stainton see to booking the Mason's in and arrange for solicitors to be present for interviews tomorrow morning.'

Cornell walked along the path to the graveyard and made his way to the grave of Martin Brown. The body of Stephanie Peston had been removed from it and placed on a tarpaulin alongside the grave for an initial examination. It would be placed in a body bag later for transportation to the lab.

A man standing by the church's lich gate caught Cornell's eye. It was James Lockheed. Cornell walked towards him.

'Is it Stephanie?' Lockheed asked.

'Subject to official identification. Probably have to use dental records, the body is too decomposed for facial recognition, but we are sure it is her. Why are you here, Mr Lockheed?'

'She was once my wife. I loved her. Took me a while to get over her leaving. Whatever she became, she didn't deserve being shoved into someone else's grave. When her body is finally released, chief inspector, I would like to give her a proper burial here in this graveyard. I will pay for it.'

'I will mention that to the coroner, but I understand this graveyard is full up.'

'For new graves, yes, but some families like ours have their own plots. My father purchased ours years ago. Stephanie was a Lockheed for only a little while, but she was a Lockheed none the less. I would like her to be buried amongst us.'

A youth came through the lich gate. It was Dennis Percival.

'Hello Dennis, what can I do for you?' said Cornell.

The young man was acting sheepishly.

'I was wondering if I should cut the grass, sir. I came to see the vicar, but there's policeman at the vicarage door who told me to get lost.'

'What day do you normally cut the grass Dennis?' asked Cornell.

Lockheed stood to one side listening.

'Thursday's normally,' Percival replied.

'But the day you found Mr Dickinson wasn't a Thursday was it?'

'No, sir, but Mrs Mason asked me to cut the grass that morning. I didn't want to because it was raining. It makes such a mess on the paths and that, but she insisted.'

'Did you notice any blood on the grass Dennis?'

'No, sir. I'm too busy trying to avoid the gravestones. I've scraped the odd one before now and had to cover the marks with mud.'

'Who pays you for cutting the grass, Dennis?'
'The vicar.'

'Well the vicar will not be around for awhile. You will need to find another job, I'm afraid.'

'You ever fancied working on a farm, Dennis?' asked Lockheed.

'Yes, sir, but I was told you wouldn't want a villager working for you.'

'I don't know who told you that, but it's not true. Come to the farm this afternoon and I'll show you around. If you don't like it, well nothing's lost.'

Percival's eyes lit up.

'Yes, sir. Thank you, sir.'

'And don't call me, sir.'

'No, sir. I'll see you later.'

Cornell and Lockheed watched as the boy left the graveyard with a bounce in his step.

'Well done,' said Cornell.

'I may regret it. The lad's not the size of two penneth of copper. But if he stays, I'll put some muscle on his back and shoulders.'

'What's the situation with you, the bull and the police?' asked Cornell.

'Made a statement last night with your Inspector Stewart. She is going to speak to the CPS and get back to me in due course. The fact the incident happened on my land may be in my favour, also the woman being armed and brandishing a weapon should also help.'

'I hope it works out for you,' said the chief inspector.

Cornell went to the *Sword and Lance* to collect his overnight bag and Rex.

'You've found this Stephanie woman in an old grave then?' enquired the landlord, polishing the tables in readiness for opening time.

'Yet to be identified, but almost certainly it's her,' replied Cornell.

'And was that the vicar and his wife in handcuffs?'

'You have great eyesight, Bill, considering you can't see the graveyard from here.'

Walton looked a bit embarrassed. He had obviously been watching the operation at the church along with a great number of villagers.

'You got me there, chief inspector.'

'Bill, it's time to say goodbye. Thanks for looking after my dog this morning and for the hospitality and humour during our stay.'

'You're welcome. How much do you want for the dog?' he asked.

Cornell laughed.

'You couldn't afford him, Bill, believe me.'

'Bring him to see me sometime, will you? He's a good dog and there's a meal here for you and a friend,' then added, 'reduced rates.'

CHAPTER THIRTY FIVE

DCI Cornell joined the A1 north of Morpeth, Rex in the front, the Reverend Neville Mason sitting seat belted but unsecured in the rear.

'What's going to happen to me?' the reverend had asked at the start of the journey.

'You are not getting out of this smelling of roses, vicar. You conspired with your wife, a murderer, to cover up the death of Stephanie Peston, or Lockheed, nee Woods as she once was. You also knew your wife murdered James Dickinson, but you kept quiet about it. That will put you in prison for a while. But you tell me everything and we can tell the judge you cooperated. May get you a few years off, but being a man of the cloth, you know you need to tell me everything anyway. It's one thing you going to jail, reverend, but when you get up there,' Cornell pointed skyward, 'you don't want Saint Peter pointing you in the direction of the other place, do you?'

'Thank you, chief inspector. You have been very kind.'

'You may not think so when the verdict comes in.'

So, recording the conversation on his smartphone, Rex sitting in the passenger seat watching the outside world pass by, the Reverend Neville Mason told Cornell how his wife, who was gay, an admission that did not surprise Cornell, had dominated him and some of the residents of East Hewick for years.

Mason explained what happened in the village hall two years ago. How Stephanie came to be murdered and what those present did with the body. How, the night James was killed, Mavis had come home with blood on her hands. He described how she washed her hands in the kitchen sink and the water was pink. How she changed and washed her bloodied clothes. How she had put something in the top drawer of the sideboard, he discovered later was her watch with blood on the broken strap. He explained how she contacted Dennis Percival first thing the following morning.

'Why was that Neville?' asked Cornell. He felt able to call the vicar by his first name.

'Two reasons. One, cutting the grass would get rid of the obvious blood stains and two, she needed someone to find the body. That way she could keep control.'

'What about Donald Peston?' asked Cornell.

'I don't know anything about that,' the vicar replied. 'I only heard about it later from a parishioner, but I knew Mavis had done it. Why would anyone else want to kill him? Hardly anyone in the village knew him.'

Several times during the course of his testimonial the man of the cloth broke down, but by the time they turned into the police station car park, he had provided Cornell with all the information he needed.

'Why didn't you report Mavis, Neville? I find it hard to accept you didn't, you being a vicar.'

'Because I loved her.'

The Reverend Neville Mason was led into the station by Cornell and taken to the booking desk. The sergeant on duty did a double take when he saw Mason's dog collar and only just refrained from making a joke about running off with the collection.

Rex and Marian were temporarily reunited outside the RVI and she almost forgot to tell Cornell that her mother was being allowed home the following day.

Max's mother stood beside her son.

'I'll take Marian home first thing tomorrow morning, Max. She and I can do a bit dusting and hoovering before her mother arrives.'

'There's no need for that, Mam.'

'Don't be daft, it's all arranged, isn't it Marian?'

Marian nodded, although Cornell doubted she would have had much say on the subject.

TWO FEET UNDER

As they walked along the corridor towards Mabel's room on the ward, Max asked Marian how her mother was.

'She's fine physically, but still can't speak. I'm worried Max.'

On entering the corridor leading to the ward, the doctor who attended Mabel called to them from his open office door. He confirmed her discharge the next day, but also confirmed her voice had not returned and it now seemed unlikely it ever would. He mentioned a nurse would be along shortly with leaflets on how to cope with speech loss and how and where to learn sign language.

Cornell desisted from commenting on the latter.

Mabel was dressed and seated in a chair by the bed when they arrived and managed a smile despite having been told earlier she may never speak again.

Her visitors kissed her and Cornell's mother took the only seat, Cornell and Marian sat on the bed. Mabel lost her smile and wrote on her pad.

'*I'm sorry.*'

Apologising for not being able to speak? *Can't have that.* Cornell picked up the writing pad.

'*No need to shout,*' he wrote.

Her smile returned for a just a moment at the joke. She took back her writing pad.

'*Serious. Not funny.*'

'It's as serious as you want it to be, Mabel,' Max spoke firmly. 'You can go into a deep depression over it, take Marian down with you, lock yourself away, or you can say, "what the hell! OK, I cannot speak, so bloody what? Not my problem." And I'll be with you all the way.'

'*What are you saying?*' she wrote, looking at him with suspicion, Marian and his mother displaying anticipatory expressions.

'I've solved the East Hewick murders.'

After being cursed by his mother, hit with a pillow by Marian, and himself asking, 'what?' he finally directed his attention to Mabel.

'Mabel Wainwright. Will you marry me?'

She scribbled on her writing pad. '*No.*'

Max Cornell was taken aback initially, but remembered her humour occasionally equalled his own and suddenly her expression lit up. She got out of her chair to embrace the man she loved, then wrote on her pad.

'*When?*'

'Before you lose any more of your senses,' was his response, only to be cursed further and hit with more pillows and cushions.

CHAPTER THIRTY SIX

The murder investigation team, minus David Watkins but supplemented by the chief superintendent, were seated in the incident room. Their chief inspector sat on a table in front of them, with his feet on a chair. Tom Dawson from the forensics laboratory was also present to provide the scientific data.

The team had previously been advised by Sergeant Donaldson that DC Watkins had gone home the previous evening, laid the law down and literally ordered all the relatives and the neighbour out of the house, leaving himself alone with his wife and child, hence his absence.

'On his return to work he may be a different person,' she suggested, drawing one or two comments of, "*I'll bet.*"

Cornell took to his feet and began the session by confirming who had been arrested and which officers would be interviewing the offenders.

Commencing his summary of events Cornell stated, 'This all started twenty seven years ago with the marriage of Stephanie Woods and Joseph Lockheed. A marriage, that according to Lockheed's mother, was never going to work. It was also a marriage that totally peeved James Dickinson who was madly in love with Stephanie Woods himself. It was Dickinson who started the rumours regarding Joseph Lockheed abusing Stephanie and it was Dickinson who chased after Stephanie so much after she left Lockheed, that she moved away.

'Stephanie Lockheed went to live in Darlington with an aunt, got a job then found a new husband, Donald Peston. They moved to Newton Aycliffe, but Peston didn't want her to work. According to those who knew her, the reason for that was because Peston wanted children and required Stephanie to stay at home and look after them. But they never did have children and Stephanie, left at home with nothing to do, started drinking. The marriage deteriorated, then two years ago she suddenly developed the urge to see her children from her first marriage and she left her Newton Aycliffe home and set off for East Hewick.

'We know all this from the Lockheed family and the Darlington and Newton Aycliffe police. Lesley Jamieson helped us out with the next bit as did the previous tenant of the *Sword and Lance,* William Cash. Stephanie arrived at the pub on a Friday afternoon and arranged to meet her daughters on the Saturday evening in the village hall. Unfortunately, Stephanie had a few drinks on the Saturday afternoon and the evening meeting did not go according to plan, resulting in the twins walking away.

'Now the Reverend Mason's testimony comes into play. Stephanie remained at the village hall that evening and continued to drink. James Dickinson, a regular at the village hall bar on a Saturday, decided to renew his desire for Stephanie. She would have none of it. Got drunker and drunker and James got sloppier and sloppier. It was now late in the evening and only a few of the villagers remained drinking. James was making a fool of himself and annoying Mavis Mason. A slanging match developed between James, Mavis and Stephanie, which then became physical resulting in Stephanie Peston throwing punches at Mavis. Then there was a free for all which ended when Stephanie was noticed lying on the floor of the village hall, blood pumping from her neck and chest with Mavis standing over her, knife in hand.

'Mavis immediately took control. Stephanie was quite dead, one of the stab wounds must have gone right through her heart. The police were not going to be contacted. She had a good idea of what to do with the body. Bury it. So, in the early hours of the Sunday morning, Stephanie Peston was buried unceremoniously by a few villagers, two feet down in the grave of Martin Brown, deceased 1931. After levelling off the ground and disposing of the soil displaced by Stephanie's body, the bowling club's groundsman, Nicolas Wordsworth, sowed commercial, fast growing and very expensive fine grass seed on the grave top. It would be green again in a matter of days.'

'How could Mavis Mason be sure the residents involved would not talk, sir?' asked DC Fielding.

'She couldn't, but a five hundred quid bribe every now and again helped.'

'I'm curious to know why Mavis was carrying a knife,' queried Ian Dennison.

'Whatever else she was, she was a bloody good gardener. I've seen the vicarage garden. Reverend Neville told me she had cut some flowers for the church before they left for the village hall and had obviously kept the knife on her.'

'So, why was James Dickinson killed, sir?' queried DC Irene Stainton.

'James had been so infatuated with Stephanie when they were teenagers that seeing her again when she returned made him firmly believe he had a chance with her. Her death in the village hall unsettled him to the extent that he developed a hatred for Mavis Mason and defied her by putting flowers on the grave where his one true love was interred. Mavis thought this would attract suspicion and had it out with him in the graveyard, catching him in the act. It ended with his death. Not having the tools or the manpower to bury him, she dragged him elsewhere in the graveyard and arranged for Dennis Percival to find the body. James may have been still alive when he was dragged, as Mavis's watch was damaged in the process.

'She attacked Doctor Wainwright when she saw her inspecting the grave of Martin Brown. She watched on as Mabe…. err, Doctor Wainwright phoned me then took the opportunity to kill her before I got there. Fortunately, she didn't succeed but she has left Doctor Wainwright unable to speak.'

'What about Donald Peston?' the chief superintendent asked, as he thought he had better contribute to the session.

'Donald and Stephanie's marriage had broken down, perhaps because they didn't have children, or, maybe because of her drinking. We don't know. But what we do know is that he had a million pound life insurance on her and needed to know her situation. When she couldn't be found, he must have been worried for his investment, so he came to her birthplace to find her. He had guessed right, East Hewick was where she had gone, but she was not there anymore. Because no one would talk to him, I think he must have suspected that Stephanie was dead, but in order to submit a claim to the insurance company he would have to show proof of her death.

'Peston tried to get close to Dickinson, offering to act for him in a totally vexatious custody case for his granddaughter. It may even have been Peston who suggested it. We know from his computer notes that he believed Dickinson knew something about Stephanie's disappearance, and he was right. Mavis knew about Peston making enquiries about Stephanie, and his apparent friendship with Dickinson, and decided he was getting too close and had to go as well.'

'Often the case,' proffered Chief Superintendent Blakeshaw, with no explanation for his comment.

'So,' interjected Sergeant Laura Donaldson, ignoring the chief superintendent, 'Donald Peston was still alive when we first arrived at East Hewick. Pity we didn't know about him then. Do we have any DNA connecting Mavis Mason to his murder?'

'None so far,' said Tom Mawson. 'Only evidence is the way he was killed and the weapon used.'

'Hopefully, that will be enough, alongside the evidence of Dickinson's killer,' stated Cornell.

'What made you suspect Mavis Mason, sir?'

'Being a keen gardener and out in the fresh air a lot of the time, she developed a good sun tan. When I first met her it was raining and although I knew about the broken watch strap, she was wearing a rugby shirt which covered her wrists. Had she not been wearing a top with long sleeves, I may have put two and two together then, but I didn't. After attacking Doctor Wainwright, she went to the rectory to wash and change, returning to join the bystanders wearing a short sleeved shirt. I didn't spot the whiteness on her wrist left by losing her watch, in the photo on DC Stainton's phone because the image was too small. It was only when I uploaded the photo to the laptop and zoomed in that I was able to spot it. Then I recalled Doctor Wainwright thinking it could have been a woman who attacked her at the graveside. It was a woman who made enquiries of her at Wansbeck General Hospital, and the officer at the RVI thought the person asking for her could also have been a woman. Mavis Mason is a big lass, not the most feminine looking of ladies and according to her husband, is gay, with a tendency to wear male clothing.'

DC Fielding interrupted.

'I recall seeing the vicar and his wife out walking the evening DCI Cornell and I were to meet Mrs Telford, who had asked us to call. I now believe the Mason's were returning from threatening Mrs Telford to keep her mouth shut.'

'I don't disagree with that,' returned Cornell.

'Had Mrs Mason got to Doctor Wainwright in hospital, do you think she would have gone as far as killing her?' asked DC Dennison.

'I think she would have. Mavis Mason is a psychopath who according to her husband, could be completely relaxed, chilled and laid back on the one hand, but capable of the worst kinds of raging temper if she was challenged in any way. By the time she had killed Peston she had become quite mad and when she saw Doctor Wainwright poking around Stephanie's burial place, she knew she had to take immediate action to prevent the secret being revealed. But she failed. She knew Doctor Wainwright wasn't dead when taken to hospital, so was a loose end that had to be taken care of. Mavis didn't know that by this time we suspected Stephanie was buried in Martin Brown's grave, otherwise there would have been no need to silence Doctor Wainwright.'

'It's difficult to imagine,' said Irene Stainton, 'how one person could have such a hold on a whole village.'

'I agree,' returned Cornell. 'People got caught up in the murder of Stephanie Peston and instead of informing the authorities, settled for covering up the crime. They may have been decent people before the incident, but accepted bribes to keep quiet afterwards. This includes Agnes Cartwright and her daughter who were at the village hall dance and witnessed the murder.'

'I got to like Agnes,' said DC Fielding. 'I wonder if what she knew got too much for her and brought on early dementia?'

'Who knows?' responded Cornell. 'She'll probably be put into some institution for the remainder of her life.'

'What is certain,' said Sergeant Donaldson, 'East Hewick will never be the same again. Better or worse, I don't know.'

Later that morning DCI Cornell and CS Blakeshaw gave a press conference. It went reasonably well until Jed Temperly of the Chronicle stood and identified himself.

'Tell us, chief inspector, are you and Doctor Wainwright intending to influence the prosecution on this occasion as well?'

The chief superintendent was about to answer, but Cornell held his arm.

'As far as I'm concerned, Mr Temperly, the answer is no, but I can't speak for Doctor Wainwright. You will have to ask her, but please be patient with her, as the attack on her life has left her unable to speak.'

Jed Temperly sat down. Doctor Wainwright's prognosis had so far not been released to the public and learning of her loss of speech obviously shocked some reporters. Several turned towards Temperly and uttered defamatory comments. Chief Superintendent Blakeshaw took that point to be an opportune moment to close the press conference.

As they were walking back upstairs, Blakeshaw was going to ask his chief inspector how he was able to think of the most appropriate answer to Temperley's question instead of blasting the man for being so insensitive, but refrained. Instead he asked Cornell, 'How did you know Lockheed was not the murderer? He would have been the first one arrested if I'd been SIO.'

'Didn't want to pick on the obvious and make the case around them, sir. When you do that, you are often wrong, then it's sometimes too late to find the real murderer. Oh, before I forget, we need to chat about Martin Fielding's disciplinary case. I think the decision is unsafe. Goodnight, sir.'

Cornell left his chief superintendent shaking his head. On the one hand the chief inspector needed bringing down a peg or two, on the other, he was a really likeable guy. Blakeshaw would like to be his friend. Maybe they could have a drink together sometime.

CHAPTER THIRTY SEVEN

After all the interviews had been completed, Cornell finally left for home, but not before having a celebratory can of John Smith's with his team. He was in the police car park about to leave when he received a call from the chief constable's personal assistant.

'The chief constable would like to see Detective Chief Inspector Cornell immediately.'

'Tomorrow not do?'

'No, it would not.'

'Can't she ring me? Perhaps if you showed her how to make a phone call, she could speak to me directly when I answered. Probably mean you would lose your job though.'

'Do I tell the chief constable you are refusing her invitation?'

Cornell almost said yes, but he would have to answer to an insubordination charge of some description.

'Tell her I will be there in ten minutes.'

She kept him waiting in her reception area for fifteen minutes, his frustration growing. Finally, he addressed the chief constable's P.A.

'Tell the chief constable I was here, waited fifteen minutes, couldn't wait any longer and will see her at a later date.'

Cornell stood to leave when a buzzer sounded on the PA's desk.

'She will see you now.'

The PA opened and held the door for Cornell to enter the office of the chief constable. He stood to attention in front of her desk. A desk that was covered in documentation. He was not asked to take a seat.

'Why is it, Detective Chief Inspector Cornell, that of all my senior officers, you give me the most problems?'

'I don't, ma'am, you just make it seem that way.'

'How dare you!' She raised her voice. 'Who the bloody hell do you think you are talking to, chief inspector?' She stood as if to emphasise her point. 'You show no respect for your seniors. There are many complaints about your conduct. You make derogatory remarks against senior lawyers and now, an old girlfriend is killed in your presence during an entirely different murder investigation ..... Why are you grinning?'

'Just that every time I solve a murder, ma'am, I end up here getting a bollicking.'

'Language, chief inspector.'

'Sorry, ma'am. I meant arse kicking.'

'You are incorrigible, aren't you?'

'Err, what's incorrigible mean, ma'am?'

The chief constable sat down, trying to maintain a straight face.

'In your case, impossible. How is Doctor Wainwright?'

'She is being allowed home, ma'am, but her voice has not yet returned and it may never.'

'That is very sad. You do know that if she doesn't regain her voice, she will lose her job?'

'I suspect that will be so, but why are we discussing Doctor Wainwright, ma'am?'

'Because I understand from the testimony you gave at the Symonds trial, that you and she are good friends.'

'Yes, ma'am.'

There was pause. The chief constable looked at her watch.

'I have an appointment in ten minutes. That's all, chief inspector.'

'Yes, ma'am. Thank you, ma'am.'

Cornell about turned and was almost at the door.

'Oh! And well done with your arrests. A vicar's wife, eh? You just never can tell, can you?'

'No, ma'am.'

'And give my best to Mabel, won't you?'

'Yes, ma'am.'

'And Max,' said the chief constable as he was about to close the door. 'Good luck.'

He wondered, as he walked down the stairs to the ground floor, why the chief constable couldn't have just emailed him.

He travelled home to Cullercoats. Mabel would be at her home by now, but he was not going to see her this evening. He wanted time with his dog and to reflect on whether his proposal to Mabel had been sensible and not just because he felt sorry for her. He didn't want to think about work, love, potential step daughters and whether he was being followed. After two miles of travel along the coast road, he ascertained he was not.

He smiled to himself recalling the very short visit with the chief constable. She was always complaining about his unique approach to policing, when in fact no one bent the rules more than she did.

He unlocked the front door of his Cullercoats home allowing his dog in before him, having retrieved the German Shepherd from being looked after for the day by his neighbour. He could tell Jenny Laidlaw had cleaned and tidied for him, for which he was extremely grateful. He could smell the furniture polish she used.

TWO FEET UNDER

Rex, after drinking water from his bowl, went into the hallway and sought his leash, dropping it in front of Cornell then sitting down. It was as if he was giving his master time to reflect on his request for a walk.

'Alright, lad. We'll have a look down the beach. But Cullercoats this time. I haven't the energy for Whitley Bay.'

The dog picked the leash up off the floor and placed it in Cornell's hand, then trotted to the front door.

BOOKS BY THIS AUTHOR

AT REST AT LAST
https://www.amazon.co.uk/dp/B07MBQDRRD

Tells the story of a young wife who loses her life in a road traffic accident in a remote village in North Northumberland to a hit and run vehicle. The car and its occupants are later identified but the police are only able to bring minor traffic charges against them. The husband does not believe his dead wife will ever be at rest until justice is properly served. From the family farm in Northumberland to the deserts of Iraq, and over a period of twenty-five years, all occupants of the vehicle are traced by the husband who delivers his own kind of judgement. A police officer and distant relative whose advances were rejected by the wife before she was married, is driven to gather evidence against the husband to settle family scores and satisfy his ego.

DEATH FACTORY
https://www.amazon.co.uk/dp/B093DT65LJ

Involves a solicitor who takes on the might of organised crime. After his pregnant girlfriend is forced to move away by her father, and he is unable to trace her whereabouts, he crosses paths with a local businessman with links to racketeering. His girlfriend then resurfaces but is firmly entangled with the crime syndicate. When he learns she is in serious trouble he is forced to return from Greece where he has found new love, to care for the daughter he has never met. He learns he has been left documents by his ex, incriminating various members of the crime organisation. Up against professional hitmen and a crooked police superintendent obstructing investigations, our solicitor persuades police officers and acquaintances of dubious credentials to assist him in ending the organised law breaking so he can return to Greece.

LICENSED FOR VENGEANCE
https://www.amazon.co.uk/dp/B091BB52LS

The sequel to Death Factory where we find our solicitor now married and living an idyllic life on a Greek island. When the drug cartel's assassination attempt on him goes badly wrong and someone close dies instead, he embarks on a mission to find those responsible. To assist with his purpose, he reunites with a clandestine organisation that possesses extraordinary powers and who are taxed with smashing organised crime. But as they close in on the cartel's leadership, the solicitor's daughter is kidnapped in retaliation and his attention becomes focused on finding and rescuing her. Another hard hitting, no nonsense thriller with a twist in the tale.

THE STONEMASON
https://www.amazon.co.uk/dp/B09JHDN2RZ

Bullied by his elder brother and discovering he is illegitimate, Ross Williams leaves home for London. He joins the police force and ultimately becomes the leader of an armed response unit.
When a drug fuelled youth goes on a shooting spree in a supermarket, Williams' squad is despatched, but with a new leader. However, Williams is forced to assume control which instigates a sequence of events that impacts on the rest of his life.
He leaves the force and eventually returns to his native Northumberland where he inherits a dilapidated estate and title from his real father. Over a period of years he and his wife improve and develop the estate and its many offshoots into thriving businesses, yet, he is bedevilled with the past and the appearance of those who would do him and his family harm, coupled with unavoidable issues that continuously arise to test his resolve.

TWO FEET UNDER

RING OF SHAME
https://www.amazon.co.uk/dp/B09Z9G7P9Y

It's a January morning and the body of a young woman, shoeless and unsuitably attired for winter, is found dead in the freezing waters of a seaside town's harbour. She has no identification and no one has reported her missing.
Did she jump, or was she pushed? Who is she?
Three days later another young woman's body, similarly dressed, is discovered in a different location. But are the two deaths linked?
Detective Chief Inspector Max Cornell thinks they are and have died for the same reason. But how does he begin the investigation when faced with interference from his superior, no witnesses, clues or evidence?

A gripping crime mystery set in Newcastle and Northumberland

DOUGLAS JOHN KNOX

ABOUT THE AUTHOR

Douglas John Knox is best known for his action packed mystery thrillers, including the DCI Max Cornell series. Mostly set in the North East of England, but his tales can take you off to the capital and overseas.

Although blessed with a colourful imagination, Douglas didn't start writing fiction until he retired from the Civil Service in 2005. It was then, with a compulsion to record his creations instead of just dreaming them, that he was stimulated to write.

Once a resident of County Durham, Douglas John Knox now lives in North Northumberland, the setting for many of his novels.
When not writing, Douglas enjoys fly fishing and tying his own fishing flies, gardening, which includes tending a large allotment and painting, both in watercolours and oils.
Also known to have the occasional glass of red wine.

Printed in Great Britain
by Amazon